Darcy Goes to War

A Novel

By

Mary Lydon Simonsen

D1738634

Quail Creek Publishing LLC

www.austenauthors.net
http://marysimonsenfanfiction.blogspot.com

Printed in the United States of America
Published by Quail Creek Publishing, LLC
quailcreekpub@hotmail.com

©2012 Quail Creek Publishing LLC
ISBN 13: 978-0615689487
ISBN 10: 0615689485

Prologue

Too exhausted to bail, the water seeped into the dinghy, soaking the inside of his wool-lined boots and fleece flight jacket. With teeth chattering and wracked by convulsions, he decided he could not get any wetter or colder and thought he might be better off if he slipped over the side. He had finally resolved to make his move when he heard a voice advising against it. A few minutes later, he saw the searchlight of an approaching ship.

Chapter 1

April 1944

Moving apace with a gust of wind at her back, Elizabeth Bennet went into The Hide and Hare carrying a crate of vegetables she was "donating" to the owners of the public house. Because she had been sitting in traffic for most of the afternoon in a lorry whose heater hadn't worked in months, she was chilled to the bone.

While picking up her load at a farm near Cambridge, no one had warned her that the whole of the U.S. Army was on the move or that they were all heading south in the direction of the Channel ports by way of her destination, the village of Meryton. The thought that the long-awaited invasion of France might actually be around the corner sent a chill through her body. *As if I wasn't cold enough*, she thought.

After fighting traffic for three hours, Lizzy eased her way out of the queue and pulled up in front of The

Hide and Hare, a mid-nineteenth century pub set in a wooded area on the outskirts of Meryton proper. Hopefully, while she was eating her dinner, the convoy would have snaked its way through the village, and she would be able to get back on the road. Upon entering the pub, Lizzy waited for her eyes to adjust to the pub's dim interior, partly because of austerity measures and partly because the walls and beams of the pub had been blackened by generations of cigarette and coal smoke and grease from its kitchen. After making out the figure of the proprietor, she headed in his direction.

"Hello, Miss Elizabeth!" Stan Corker bellowed. "You look half frozen. I'd offer you a cuppa, but we're all out of tea. It will have to be coffee and watered down at that."

"A cup of coffee would be lovely, Stan, and whatever you have left over from lunch." She only hoped it wasn't pea soup. No one ever seemed to run out of that. Lizzy explained that she had been trying to get to the Meryton depot by way of every back road between Cambridge and the pub, but was meeting a Yank at every turn.

"Oh, to be sure, it's a mess out there," Stan acknowledged. "The Americans sent a liaison officer around here on Tuesday telling us they would be coming through in long convoys, snarling up traffic and making life miserable for the locals. He warned us that more than a few of their lads would try to sneak in here for a pint while the convoys inched their way through the village," he said, jerking his head in the direction of a covey of Americans hovering together at the end of the bar. "'Boys will be boys' is what I said, and their money's good in here."

"You got more warning than I did then," Lizzy said, inhaling the hot coffee. "If I had known about the convoys, I would have stayed in Cambridge for a few more hours instead of wasting my petrol. I've been idling half the day."

Because an American MP had allowed her to squeeze in behind a truck full of infantrymen, Lizzy had not lacked for entertainment. Before turning into the drive for the public house, the GIs had serenaded her with *Deep in the Heart of Texas* and *Home on the Range* and had sent her on her way with cheers and blown kisses.

"Lucky lads. Looking at a pretty girl instead of the mug of some dogface." After checking to see if anyone was listening, Stan asked, "What have you got for me today?" If he was lucky, Lizzy would have some asparagus or broad beans. He just hoped it wasn't peas or cabbage. He was sick to death of pea soup and cabbage soup.

"Along with the usual peas, garlic, and onions, I am transporting the most beautiful spears of asparagus you have seen since Britain went to war over Poland. They were handpicked by Land Girls from the East End. With their cockney accents, I could hardly understand them. It's hard to believe we were all speaking English."

"I wouldn't call what they speak English." Looking over his shoulder, Stan shouted to his cook to make a fresh batch of fish and chips for the lovely Elizabeth Bennet. "Before I forget, thank you for the contraband. You won't get into trouble, now will you?"

Lizzy shook her head. "It's very important that your patrons eat a balanced diet," she answered, knowing that the food served at The Hide and Hare was of marginal interest to its customers for many reasons, but mostly because of the taste. It seemed as if salt was the only seasoning known to the cook.

"I see your trade hasn't dropped off," Lizzy added, as she looked around the pub, seeing a fairly robust crowd.

"Nor am I expecting it to. We'll still have the Yanks from the Nuthampstead Airbase coming in, but our lads will be in here as well. It seems the old Royal Air Force station at Helmsley that the Americans took over late in '42 has been handed back to a new RAF bomber group. They've been gracing us with their presence for about two weeks now," Stan said, gesturing in the direction of some RAF officers huddled over their pints in a nearby booth. "The big wigs at Bomber Command decided to mix some of the veterans with replacements and retrain them here at Helmsley. There's been a fair amount of grumbling about it by that lot."

"Well, seasoned crews never want to take on inexperienced men, now do they?" she said, thinking of her own training period as a lorry driver with her less than cordial trainer.

"No, and I take their point. Right now they're doing a lot of takeoffs and landings and short hops to France and Holland."

"I'll be glad when it's all over," Lizzy said, a statement she had been making since the shooting had started four years earlier. "While you see to my dinner, I'm going to call on a man named 'John,'" she said with a wink.

As Lizzy made her way to the rear of the pub and the lavatory, Stan's wife called her over, and Lizzy knew what would happen next. Nancy Corker would tell the officers that here was one of the prettiest girls in Hertfordshire and an excellent dancer as well and wasn't there a dance coming up a week Saturday at Helmsley? Hint. Hint.

"Yes, there is a dance, Mrs. Corker, but I am working that night. I will be the one collecting the girls at the church in my lorry and driving them to the station. We must have dance partners for our men in service to keep up their morale," she answered, smiling.

"But surely you will be parking the lorry and having a dance yourself?" Mrs. Corker asked.

"Possibly," Lizzy said almost in a whisper. She hated these situations, but because she was twenty-three, unmarried, not bad to look at, and with no serious romantic interest in her life, she was always being singled out by the well-intentioned matrons of Meryton as someone who needed help in finding a date even though the countryside had more available Yanks in it than cows or cornstalks, and she could have had the pick of the crop.

"Are you planning to go to the dance, Darcy?" one of the men asked an officer who was more interested in his brew than Lizzy's prospects for a partner. Although Darcy didn't seem interested, her beautiful dark curls and ebony eyes weren't lost on the man who was doing the asking, and it was obvious he was angling for a dance himself.

"No, I won't be going to the dance, Rogers," Darcy finally answered. "I already had that experience the first week I was here—joint American and British effort—passing the baton sort of thing when the station changed hands."

"Well, sir, we can boast some of the finest looking girls in the county hereabouts, and here's one to prove it," Mrs. Corker said, pushing Lizzy forward. "Don't hide your light under a bushel, dear. All of these men are *officers*," she whispered.

"Excuse me. I need to use the...," and Lizzy jerked her head in the direction of the loo, but as she squeezed past the chubby matron, she heard the dark-haired officer remark, "Rogers, I shall warn you there is little beauty in the girls who attend these dances, and they aren't exactly light on their feet. If you do go to the dance, my advice is to wear your jump boots."

"That was unkind, sir," Mrs. Corker said, chastising the surly gentleman, but he gave no indication he had heard her.

When Lizzy came out of the lavatory, she avoided all eye contact with the members of the RAF and was happy to find her meal waiting for her. While Lizzy ate, Stan talked.

"Don't be paying any mind to what that dark-haired fellow had to say. I have it on good authority that he was on the Nuremburg raid last month. Did you read about that one, Lizzy? Near one hundred planes shot down. I'm told he got his crew home, as the Americans say, on a wing and a prayer, but two of them were shot up and died in hospital. Of course, something like that would sour anyone's mood, and now he's being forced to put a bunch of recruits through the paces. He took a group out last night for a milk run to France. Actually, I'm just guessing it was France, but they weren't gone long enough to pay Herr Hitler a visit."

"A milk run is it, Stan? You are beginning to

sound like a Yank yourself," Lizzy said, avoiding the more serious subject of the RAF's costliest raid of the war. "Please don't let me hear you calling football 'soccer' or it might affect our friendship."

"I'd have a riot in here if ever I did," Stan said, laughing. "But it would be hard not to pick up some of the Yanks' jargon, what with them in here all the time singing their songs and telling their stories and stealing our girls. Did you hear that Nancy's niece is to be married to an American? Damn foolish thing to do with the invasion just around the corner and him being in the airborne division and all, but there's a reason for the hurried marriage, if you take my meaning."

Lizzy did take his meaning, but there wasn't a soul in the village who would be surprised to learn Amanda Thorpe was pregnant. The surprise was that it hadn't happened sooner.

"Well, let's hope that that particular officer has a ride back to the base," Lizzy said, refusing to comment on Nancy Corker's niece. "I imagine when he finally stands up, he'll find he doesn't have the use of his legs."

"Oh, don't worry about him. That young officer who was looking you over will see him to the lorry that takes the lot of them back to the base. He won't be flying tomorrow or he wouldn't be in here, so he'll have a whole day to sleep it off."

After cleaning her plate, Lizzy reached into her pocket to pay the tab, but Stan told her to put her money away. "You've had a long day, and this is my way of saying thank you for driving around the country in that beat-up lorry and for not getting your back up about that officer's comments."

"I'll probably never see him again, so it would really be a waste of my time, now wouldn't it? Besides, I don't want him to think his barb hit its mark."

"There you go, lass. Good attitude wins the day every time or that's what the missus tells me."

Lizzy told Stan that she didn't think she would be back in The Hide and Hare until the Yank convoys were off the road. "Because the Americans don't like driving on the left side, they drive right down the middle of the road so you can't get past them. But I'm not complaining. What would we do without them?"

"Or those chaps over there as well."

"Of course. We shouldn't take our boys for granted even the less pleasant ones. Well, I best be off."

As she was putting her coat on, the dark-haired lieutenant looked up from his drink and stared at her, and kept on staring, as if trying to place her, but Lizzy was sure she would have remembered meeting someone as good looking as he was—or as rude. It was only after giving her the most quizzical expression that he finally looked away.

"*Cheeky*," Lizzy thought, and after buttoning her coat, she stepped into the night.

Chapter 2

"You're late," Mrs. Bennet said as soon as Lizzy walked through the kitchen door. "I couldn't hold dinner any longer, and you have mud on your trousers," she grumbled as she took the asparagus bundled up in last week's newspaper from her second eldest daughter. "More work for me."

"More work because of the asparagus or the trousers?" Lizzy asked.

"Don't you be flippant with me, young lady. I'm in no mood."

"Mum, I told you if I wasn't home by 7:00 that you should have dinner without me," Lizzy said after stepping over the threshold of the mudroom. While she brushed away the dirt clinging to her trousers, she reminded her mother that there was no way for her to know what time she would be home as she never knew where she was being sent. "Because the Americans are clogging the roads, I didn't get the lorry back to the depot until after 7:00."

"Americans! I should have known," she

harrumphed. Mrs. Bennet did not dislike Americans, but on this particular day, she was prepared to pick a fight with someone—anyone. "Truth to tell, you wouldn't have these problems if you weren't driving a lorry. Why can't you get a job like Jane working for your father?"

Lizzy said nothing because her mother already knew the answer. The National Service Act stated that a magistrate with Mr. Bennet's caseload would be allotted one secretary and one law clerk. Because Jane already had experience working for Papa in his law practice, it made sense for her to take the position.

"I could be with Mary on Malta firing an ack-ack gun," Lizzy said, trying to lighten the mood.

"But that worked out for her, now didn't it? She has a beau."

"Who has a beau?" Kitty Bennet asked as she entered Longbourn's kitchen.

"Mary has a beau!" Mrs. Bennet barked. "If you took the time to read your sister's letters, you would know she is seeing an RAF mechanic who is stationed on the island."

"My goodness!" Kitty said, shocked to hear "Mary" and "beau" mentioned in the same sentence. "Well, that's wonderful for her, and for us too, because now she will have something interesting to write about other than firing her gun and the noble

Maltese who braved German bombs day after day after day," Kitty said, rolling her eyes. "I wonder if you stay on the island long enough if you end up looking like a Maltese, you know, those little fluffy white dogs?"

"Sometimes you are the silliest girl, Kitty," her mother grumbled, "and silly girls wash the dishes."

"But I…"

"I'll wash and you wipe," Lizzy said, jumping in quickly in the hope of avoiding an argument.

"I am going upstairs," Mrs. Bennet said, "and I do not wish to be disturbed."

After their mother left the kitchen, Kitty, the second youngest Bennet daughter, explained why their mother was out of sorts: Their sister Lydia had received a letter from the Ministry of Labor. Because she was now eighteen, Lydia was old enough to be conscripted for war work. Although the letter had been expected, it did not make it any easier for Mrs. Bennet to let go of her youngest daughter.

"I don't understand why Mum is so upset," Kitty said, "I already told her that Lydia will be working with me at the uniform factory."

"How do you know that?" Lizzy asked. "She hasn't had her interview yet." Lizzy remembered her own interview. Because she was unmarried, she was considered to be "mobile" and could be sent anywhere in Great Britain, including farms and factories. But when she told the interviewer she knew how to drive a lorry, she was assigned to the Meryton depot, much to everyone's relief, including her own.

"Because Mr. Greer fixed it with the review board," Kitty answered. "He says things go much smoother when the girl is local and has someone she knows working beside her."

"Yes," Lizzy said, nodding. "I can see the logic in that."

"I keep telling Mum it could be so much worse. Letitia Moreland was assigned to the Dickinson munitions factory in Hemel Hempstead and lives in a dormitory, and there's always the chance Lydia could be assigned farm work," Kitty said, shuddering at the thought. "Besides, Lydia is thrilled to bits with her assignment because it puts her very near to the American airbase with the Yanks and all their money."

There was no doubt Lydia could see the logic in that!

"By the way, where is Lydia?"

"She's at Maria Lucas's house pretending to study for her exit exams, but she's really..."

Lizzy heard someone coming down the hall and put her finger to her lips in case it was their mother. Instead of Mrs. Bennet, Jane came through the door, and it was obvious from the look on her face that something good had happened.

"Dad's calling for his tea," Jane said while putting the kettle on the stove. "Kitty, I'll take over for you. I have to wait for the kettle to boil anyway."

After Kitty was safely out of the room, Jane burst out with the remarkable news that she had met a man at the Helmsley canteen, a hangar-like building that was a part of the Helmsley station, but one conveniently located outside the chain-link fencing erected by the Americans. It was very near to the Meryton depot, and because her bicycle had gone missing from the depot while she had been out on a delivery, Lizzy now parked it in the canteen's supply shed.

"Because Papa had a late appointment, I walked to the canteen to have my dinner. When Mrs. Dickens told me you were expected at any time, I decided to wait so that you and I could walk home together."

"Expected at any time? How could Mrs. Dickens possibly know that? *I* don't even know when I'll get to the canteen."

"Lizzy, that's not important right now. What is important is that I met a man!"

"You met a man? At the canteen?" Lizzy asked, feigning surprise. "Why that's almost as rare as finding feathers on a duck."

"But this was a very particular man," Jane answered, ignoring her sister's sarcasm. "Do you remember that Netherfield Park was sold to some unknown buyer right before the war started?" Lizzy nodded. "The officer I met today, Mr. Charles Bingley, was the person who bought it. But because he volunteered as soon as war was declared, he has never actually lived in the house."

Netherfield Park, a lovely red-brick Georgian mansion situated on acreage abutting the Bennet property, was an integral part of the Meryton neighborhood, providing the best setting for formal dances. Despite the Darlingtons having lived at Netherfield Park for four generations, when the dark clouds of war appeared on the horizon, they had sold the house to Mr. Bingley so that they might join their daughter's family in Toronto. Early in the war, the estate had been requisitioned by the RAF for the purpose of billeting its officers. When the Americans took over Helmsley Air Station in 1943, they had used it as a billet for their officers as well. But now the RAF was back.

"Can you guess where Mr. Bingley is billeted?" But Jane didn't wait for Lizzy to answer. "Netherfield Park!"

"Oh, that is too funny," Lizzy said, agreeing with her sister.

"Mr. Bingley said he dare not tell any of his fellow officers that he owns the house or he would never hear the end of it. But here is the good news. Guests are allowed to visit with the officers in the sitting room and library, and Mr. Bingley has invited me to take tea with him after church on Sunday."

"Kudos, Jane. Nice work for an afternoon."

"Will you come with me?" Jane asked as she sautéed some asparagus in bacon grease for her father's dinner.

"I don't see why not. I don't have anything else to do on Sunday," Lizzy said as she silenced the whistling kettle.

"Excellent."

* * *

"Well, there you are, Lizzy, with my mystery dinner. What goodies fell off the back of the lorry today?" Mr. Bennet asked.

"Limp asparagus," Mrs. Bennet answered. Like a dog worrying a bone, she refused to let go of her anger over Lydia's National Service letter, something every eligible woman in Britain received near her eighteenth birthday.

"I thought you were going upstairs," Lizzy said before putting the tray down on the teacart.

"Your mother has decided to continue to grace us with her presence," Mr. Bennet answered while looking over his spectacles in his wife's direction.

"The asparagus was in tolerably good condition, and Jane was able to cut around the damaged bits," Lizzy said and received a sympathetic nod from her father. He was aware that his wife was out of sorts, not because of the less-than-perfect spears, but because her darling Lydia had been summoned to join the ranks of women working in the war effort.

"Is no one going to join me?"

"Some of us were home for dinner, Tom," Mrs. Bennet answered through pursed lips.

"My apologies, my dear, but I had some documents I needed to read regarding a nasty brawl last week at the Gray Duck involving the Australians and some disgruntled civilians fighting over a few of our local beauties. Damage was done. Chairs broken. Glass shattered. Reputations tarnished," he said, chuckling. "While I was sorting it out, I sent Jane home."

"I had a bite to eat at the canteen," Jane said, offering an explanation for having gone missing during dinner.

"And I had fish and chips at The Hide and Hare," Lizzy said, and immediately regretted sharing that information.

"Thank you for ringing to let me know you were dining out." An ill-tempered Mrs. Bennet rose and left the room.

After she heard the door to her parents' bedroom close, Jane shared her news about Mr. Bingley and Netherfield Park with her father. Because their mother was so eager for her daughters to marry, even in the midst of a war, Jane decided it was best not to mention meeting Mr. Bingley to her mother because she would have jumped from having a cup of coffee at a canteen to a courtship and, from there, to a walk down the aisle in the blink of an eye.

"I wondered why there were so many RAF officers in The Hide and Hare this evening, but if they are being billeted at Netherfield, then it makes sense," Lizzy said. "Considering their numbers, they might push the Americans right out of the pubs."

"Oh, I hope not," Kitty said.

"Why should you care?" Lizzy asked. "You aren't allowed in a pub."

Because of pub brawls and numerous incidences of public drunkenness by members of the military, Kitty, who was not yet twenty, had been told by her father that if she even thought about going into a public house, she would be confined to Longbourn for the duration of the war.

"But you were talking about the officers you met at The Hide and Hare," Kitty said, returning the conversation to the safer subject of British officers.

"Yes, some were handsome, some not so handsome, and some handsome and rude."

"Someone was rude to my Lizzy?" Mr. Bennet asked wide-eyed. "Surely not."

Lizzy acquainted her father and sisters with the disagreeable Flight Lieutenant Darcy and his unkind remarks about the lack of attractive females in Meryton, a statement Kitty agreed with—at least for those girls who had attended a dance earlier in the month.

"Mr. Darcy is probably referring to the formal dance they had at Netherfield Park a few weeks ago. Dress uniforms for the men and evening gowns for the ladies is what I heard, and the band was the RAF Squadronaires."

"How do you know all this?" Lizzy asked.

Because the uniform factory was located between the newly requisitioned RAF station and the American airbase, Kitty explained that all information regarding both air forces was funneled through the canteen at the factory. The fact that the RAF had returned to Helmsley was not news to her.

"But there are lots of pretty girls in Meryton," Lizzy answered, defending her friends.

"Yes, there *are* pretty girls in Meryton, but they weren't the ones who were invited," Kitty said. "It was Cassie Brooke and that homely freckled thing, Mary King, and Angelica Long, whose face is as long as her name, and Mrs. Drapers' two unmarried daughters. Everyone else was the wife of somebody."

"What about the Lucases?"

"Maria was invited, but she caught a stomach virus, and Charlotte didn't attend because she has set her sights on the vicar's son. I have no idea why she's interested in Mr. Collins. He thinks because he read at Oxford that he's the cat's pyjamas, but he is most definitely not. He's as plain as day and boring!" In Kitty's opinion, there were no greater sins than a man who was less than handsome and one who failed to amuse.

Unlike Kitty who judged every book by its cover, Lizzy understood Charlotte's interest in Mr. Collins. Because of extremely poor eyesight, the vicar's son had failed his physical examination and continued to serve as his father's assistant in the village church. After losing a beloved brother in the war in North Africa, Charlotte was quite content with the idea of being courted by a man who would never have to put on a uniform.

"But why weren't we invited? The Bennet sisters would certainly have dazzled them," Lizzy said, smiling at her father.

"Because Mrs. Long, Mrs. King, and Lady Lucas were in charge of the guest list, and until their daughters are married off, there never will be a Bennet daughter on any such list. Besides, they probably thought Lizzy might show up in trousers or that we would arrive in Papa's 1928 coupe." And everyone had a good laugh at Kitty's assessment.

"No reason to part with a perfectly good motor just because it has a few miles on it," Mr. Bennet answered in defense of his aging auto. "If that were the standard, I would have to trade in your mother."

"For shame, Papa," Lizzy said, wagging her finger at him.

"Do you fancy a game of cards, girls? I want to hear more about these handsome, and not so handsome, RAF officers."

Chapter 3

As she dealt the cards for a game of rummy, Lizzy asked her father if he had been aware that the RAF had returned to Helmsley. Mr. Bennet nodded.

"Even if I had not heard it from Sir William Lucas, I would have known of the RAF's return because, for the past few weeks, I have been watching Lancaster bombers fly over North Meryton and my office every day on their approach to Helmsley. I have also met up with a few of the chaps in RAF blue walking up and down High Street looking for something to do. After buying them lunch, and under probing cross examination, they revealed all. As I suspected, a fair amount of them are replacements for the boys we lost in the March raid over Nuremburg."

"It is amazing to me that the newspapers are allowed to write about such things," Jane said while drawing a card from the deck. "I am sure it is not that way in Germany."

"We still have a free press in England, my dear," her father said, picking up her discard. "As far as the people of Germany are concerned, it has been so long since they have read the truth in their newspapers or heard it on their wireless sets, they wouldn't know how to spot it. Dr. Goebbels and his propaganda machine have done their jobs well."

"Who is Dr. Gerbils?" Kitty asked.

"A veterinarian," Lizzy answered, smiling at her father. "It's your turn, Kitty."

"I still find it odd that our newspapers are not allowed to print the weather for fear it might aid the enemy," Jane continued, "but they can write that over ninety bombers were lost on one raid. I am sure Hitler did his happy dance when he read about that."

"When you lose that many men and planes, people will find out about it anyway because so many families will be getting telegrams saying that their loved ones have been killed or are missing or have been taken prisoner. You want to avoid bad news coming out in dribs and drabs. That is what happened with the Battle of the Somme when I was in the mixer in The Great War. Twenty thousand British soldiers were killed on the first day, and the powers that be thought they could keep such horrific news contained.

"Kitty, you either have the cards or you don't," her father said, tapping the table, and Kitty quickly drew a card. "You have to discard one now," her father added, an edge of impatience creeping into his voice.

"But I want to keep both of them," Kitty said, staring at her hand.

"And I want to win the Irish Lottery! Get on with it, girl."

"The RAF is hosting a dance at Helmsley a week Saturday that is open to the public," Lizzy said. "I was hoping to convince Kitty to go."

But Kitty was not in the least bit interested. Because the Americans had the best bands that played all the latest jazz numbers and served cold beer, Coca Cola, hot dogs, potato chips, and hamburgers, all of her friends wanted to go to the American dances.

"I don't want to be eating potato crisps all night while listening to a lousy band play *The White Cliffs of Dover* and that is what would happen at Helmsley."

There was no disputing Kitty's argument. Because of their access to commodities that had been in short supply for years in England, the Americans were wildly popular in the village, especially with the younger crowd. In addition to their weekly dances, the Yanks hosted a movie night. Unlike the pre-war British films that everyone had seen a dozen times or films that were little more than propaganda reels, the movies shown on the American base were the latest releases coming out of Hollywood with all its glitz, glamour, and big name stars. But even with all their enticements, it was the Americans themselves who were the major attraction. After more than four years of war, the British were tired. But the Yanks had a spring in their step and money in their pockets, and they were willing to spend it on the local girls.

"At the dance last week, an American gave me a pack of Pall Mall cigarettes. I didn't ask for it," Kitty quickly added after seeing her sisters' frowns. "I was able to trade it for nylons with one of the girls at work, and then I traded the nylons for that pretty new hair clasp I wore to church. One of the Americans bought it for his girlfriend at the Post Exchange at Nuthampstead, but she already had one from another boyfriend, so she was willing to trade."

Jane and Lizzy looked to their father. This was the perfect opportunity for him to tell Kitty that what she was doing was the same as buying contraband on the black market, not to mention one girl having two American boyfriends, but all he said was that some things never changed with an amused look on his face.

"I wish you two wouldn't look down your noses at me because I go to the dances at the American base," Kitty said. "I work hard all week in a uniform factory sewing sleeves on shirts eight hours a day. Why shouldn't I have a bit of fun on a Saturday night? Mum doesn't mind, and I always act like a lady."

There were so many reasons why Kitty shouldn't be allowed to go to the dances without her older sisters. She was a very pretty girl with an excellent figure, and she certainly filled out her sweater. Americans had well-deserved reputations for being oversexed, and with pockets full of money, they could show a girl a good time as a first step toward getting what they wanted. Kitty was also naïve and a follower. And then there was Lydia. As soon as she finished secondary school, she, too, would be allowed to go to the dances with Kitty, and there wasn't a bigger flirt in Meryton than Lydia Bennet. With Lydia out there, Lizzy's forecast was for stormy weather.

"I am not saying you shouldn't have fun, but it would make for a nice change if you went to the dance at Helmsley a week Saturday. You will see lots of new faces," Lizzy said while drawing a card.

"No, Lizzy, I don't want to go to Helmsley," Kitty answered, her voice growing more insistent. "The purpose of going to dances is to be entertained not punished."

"And no one will give you a pack of Pall Malls," Lizzy said, completely frustrated with her younger sister. After folding her hand, she said she was going to bed as she had an early start in the morning.

"You know, Lizzy, once upon a time, you were fun to be around," Kitty called after her.

Lizzy came back into the room and glared at her sister. "The men at Helmsley are British or members of the British Commonwealth, and they are fighting for our freedom and have been doing so since 1940. There's a war on, Kitty, or haven't you heard?" Lizzy turned on her heel and stormed out.

Chapter 4

After church on Sunday, Lizzy was looking forward to a quiet afternoon listening to the radio and reading the newspaper. She had forgotten all about her promise to go with Jane to Netherfield Park for tea with Mr. Bingley. Although Jane was eager to see the gentleman again, she refused to go alone. Lizzy's pleas for a quiet afternoon in front of the fire were in vain.

"It is obvious Mr. Bingley is already smitten," Lizzy said, thinking about his note *and* telephone call, "so I don't see why I have to go. Haven't you heard that 'two's company, three's a crowd?'"

"Just this one time, Lizzy, please. I am a little nervous. It's been such a long while since…"

"Yes, of course," Lizzy said, catapulting herself out of her chair.

Eighteen months earlier, Jane's fiancé, Jeremy Lucas had been killed at the battle of El Alamein in North Africa. In the eighteen months since his death, Jane had rebuffed the advances of all comers, that is, until she had met Flight Lieutenant Charles Bingley. Considering her loss, it was only natural that Jane would require some hand holding in her first foray back into the world of flirtation and romance.

The sisters traversed the three miles between Netherfield and Longbourn on foot, Jane having successfully resisted Lizzy's suggestion that they cut across the fields and shorten their trek by a quarter mile.

"It rained yesterday, Lizzy. You may not mind arriving at Netherfield Park with muddy shoes and damp stockings, but I certainly do. And why are you wearing those ugly boots?"

"As you pointed out, it rained yesterday, and there are puddles everywhere." Considering that the purpose of going to Netherfield was for Jane to meet Mr. Bingley, it really didn't matter what *she* wore.

As the sisters walked down the drive, Lizzy realized how much she loved the old Georgian mansion. When they were young, Elspeth Darlington would invite the Bennet sisters to tea in her full-sized dollhouse in the gardens, and they would dine on little china plates and sip from tiny floral teacups. Although such thoughts were premature, if Jane became Mrs. Charles Bingley, it would ensure that Netherfield Park would remain an integral part of the Meryton neighborhood, and Lizzy smiled at the thought.

After climbing the steps of the manor house, they were met by Mr. Buttons, the Darlington's butler, who had had been on staff at Netherfield since he had retired from musical theater two decades earlier. Now in his seventies, he could still tap out a tune, and it was he who had taught everyone how to do the Lambeth Walk at a dance in '38 in the old assembly hall and had outlasted people half his age. He greeted the Bennet sisters with a soft-shoe shuffle and a "shave and a haircut: five bob," and he held out his hand as if waiting for the coins to cross his palm.

"And here are the two prettiest ladies in the whole of Hertfordshire. I would go so far as to say the whole of England. Although it would be the truth, you might accuse me of exaggerating and not believe a word I said."

"How good it is to see you again, Mr. Buttons," Jane said, taking the butler's extended hand while Lizzy clasped the other. "I hope the boys aren't wearing you down."

"Oh, they are a lively group, they are—a nice change from the Americans. With the Yanks, we had only the most senior officers staying here, and, frankly, they were always on their best behavior. As one of the young aides used to say to me, 'It's Snoozeville around here.' But no longer. These young chaps keep me hopping. Please allow me to show you to the lounge, formerly known as the drawing room."

Before the party made it to the lounge, Mr. Bingley bounded into the foyer. After introductions were made, Bingley, who insisted the Bennet sisters call him Charles, escorted the ladies through the lounge and into the library. With the smell of leather and burning wood permeating the room, Lizzy was flooded by memories of the Darlingtons, all avid readers, sitting by the fire reading a newspaper or book. But then she concentrated on Charles, a handsome man of about twenty-seven with reddish brown hair and blue eyes, and his interest in Jane could hardly be missed as he could not take his eyes off of her.

"It was so good to see Mr. Buttons again," Jane began. "He is a neighborhood favorite. Everyone just adores him."

"He is a favorite here as well. I was looking out the window, and I saw the act he put on for you. In addition to being quick on his feet, Buttons is a quick thinker." Then Charles lowered his voice. "I'm very keen not to have anyone know I own this house. You can't imagine the ribbing I would have to endure if they did. But on the day I arrived here at my assigned billet, I was carrying my kit up the steps when Buttons came out and said, 'It's a pleasure to see you again, sir.' Even though, he hadn't laid eyes on me in three years, he remembered me. Hearing his greeting, my mate looked at me for an explanation, but without missing a beat, Buttons said, 'At my age, sir, I assume I have met everyone at least once.' Clever fellow, isn't he? And here's another," and Bingley called out to an officer who had just come into the library.

When Lizzy saw who it was, her back arched like an irritated cat. It was the rude man from The Hide and Hare, a person she had hoped never to see again.

"Darcy, over here," Charles said, waving frantically at his friend. "This is Miss Jane Bennet, the lady I was telling you about, and her sister, Miss Elizabeth Bennet."

"I am pleased to make your acquaintance," Darcy said with a bow of his head.

"Darcy is the grandson of the Earl of Stepton and the son of Sir David Darcy and Lady Anne Darcy. They have an estate in Derbyshire and…"

"Bingley, please," Darcy said, interrupting his friend. "An introduction does not require the history of my family."

For Lizzy, the little bit of information Charles had blurted out explained a lot about Flight Lieutenant Darcy. As the grandson of an earl, he would have been reared by nurses and governesses and would have attended the finest public schools. After leaving Cambridge or Oxford, he would have gone on a Grand Tour of the Continent, and if the war hadn't intervened, he would have chosen a wife from London's society pages and fathered three perfect children, one of whom would be his son and heir. Considering his elite background, he probably felt it was his God-given right to be rude to her or anyone beneath his station in life.

No sooner had these thoughts crossed her mind than she tried to dislodge them. Why was she being so judgmental? She had gone from zero to forty in seconds when the man had uttered only one sentence. But after thinking about how he had looked at her in The Hide and Hare, she realized that despite statements to the contrary, the man had got under her skin.

"You are the lady Bingley met at the canteen, I presume?" Darcy said, addressing Jane.

"Yes, we did meet at the canteen," Charles said, answering for Jane. "Earlier, I was telling Darcy that we talked for two hours over a plate of chips and two cups of coffee."

Darcy turned his attention to Lizzy. There was something vaguely familiar about her, and he asked if they had met before.

"I don't know. Where have you been?"

"Good answer," Bingley said, laughing, but Jane looked at her sister with a curious look. Lizzy's comment sounded accusatory.

"Hmm. I imagine not" was Darcy's only response, and he gestured for everyone to sit down.

"I gather you and Mr. Darcy are in the same squadron," Jane quickly added, covering up for her sister's remark.

"Yes, we are," Charles answered. "Had a bit of a scare today. We went down to the hall to make sure we weren't flying this evening, and there was our squadron, No. 9, on the board. Fortunately, it was a mistake. It was really No. 4; bit of chalk had smeared. But we will be going out tomorrow night. Worst luck," he said, looking at Jane.

"Before turning Helmsley over to the Americans," Jane said, "the commanding officer allowed visitors on the base, and some of us were invited to sit in the pilot's seat of a Lancaster."

"I'm sure I know why you were singled out. Prettiest girl on the tarmac," Bingley said, gushing.

"I have to say it was very tight quarters in there," Jane continued, but it was evident that she was pleased by Charles's comment. "The thing that surprised me the most was that there was no co-pilot."

"A definite design flaw," Bingley agreed, "at least in the opinions of the crew, because, in the end, the success of the mission depends on the pilot. If you don't have one, well, you have a problem."

"How long have you been flying a Lancaster?" Lizzy asked Charles.

"About a year. Before that, I flew a Stirling. I much prefer a Lanc. But Darcy's been in the game a lot longer than I have," Bingley said, trying to bring his silent friend into the conversation. "In '42, he flew a Hurricat, a specially outfitted Hurricane fighter. There's a funny story that goes with that. On his last mission…"

Darcy sat up straight in his chair as if someone had pinched him. "I shall tell you that Bingley finds more entertainment value in that tale than I do, so I shall spare you the details," he said in a tone indicating that that particular story would remain untold.

While his friend talked, Darcy studied the dark-haired beauty who had accompanied Bingley's latest romantic interest to Netherfield. It was obvious from her cutting remark and pursed lips that she didn't like him, and he wondered why. And why did she look so familiar? He was convinced that, despite her response, they had definitely met. But the particulars of their meeting remained stubbornly buried in the recesses of his mind.

"Miss Elizabeth, I believe you are familiar with this property," Darcy said. When Lizzy nodded, he asked if she would be good enough to show him the gardens.

Lizzy didn't see how she could say 'no' to a friend of Mr. Bingley's, but she was not happy about it. She found the man to be rude and abrupt, cutting Charles off mid sentence, and now she was supposed to take a stroll in the gardens with him?

Upon reaching the main gardens, Darcy explained the reason for his request. "I assume the purpose of your sister's coming here today was to spend time with Bingley?"

"Yes."

"Well, now they will have an opportunity to do so without interference."

That was all fine and good—for Jane. However, Mr. Darcy's plan left Lizzy stuck with Charles's unpleasant friend. But she would soldier on, and so she suggested they visit a fountain deeper in the gardens. However, when they reached it, they found it silent, the water having been drained.

"Of course, they wouldn't keep the fountain running during the war," Lizzy said, staring at the concrete pool with only a half inch of rainwater in it. Because of neglect, the concrete was covered with green slime. "If they don't do something about the stagnant water, they will have gnats. Actually, it's too late," Lizzy said, swatting away the first of the annoying insects. She looked at Mr. Darcy who seemed unbothered by the airborne pests. "Gnats are probably not a major concern to someone who flies bombing missions over Germany in a plane with no co-pilot, but I really don't like them."

"But that's why we fly night missions. It's top secret that there's only the one pilot," he said, putting his fingers to his lips. "So keep mum because if Jerry should find out about it, they might take advantage of the situation, and they have all those pesky night fighters out there looking for us."

Despite her dislike of Flight Lieutenant Darcy, Lizzy was enjoying his droll wit, and because the man was not a complete stick in the mud, she found the tension easing.

"I understand you live in the neighborhood," Darcy said.

"Yes, Netherfield is within walking distance of my home, and so Jane and I walked." Darcy's eyes focused on her muddied boots. Following his gaze, Lizzy added, "I wiped my boots before entering Netherfield if that is your concern."

"I didn't mean to imply... I didn't think you had," Darcy stuttered, taken aback by her comment. "Do you live on a farm?"

"Why do you ask? Is there hay in my hair?"

"No, of course not. It's just that you said your property abutted Netherfield. Netherfield is still a working farm. No offense was intended by my comment."

No offense intended this time, Lizzy thought, but then decided to change her tone. There was no excuse for rudeness—not on his part, nor hers.

"For ages, Longbourn was a farm owned by the Bennet family," she explained, "but after my grandfather died, my father, who is a magistrate in Meryton, sold most of the acreage. Having grown up on a farm, he knew enough about farming to know he didn't want to be a farmer. However, we do have six hens, a randy rooster, and a vicious goose. But the goose will get his just desserts come Christmas when he'll be the centerpiece of our holiday dinner."

"Since the start of the war, my father has put on

his farmer's hat as well," Darcy said. "In addition to his Victory garden, he also raises chickens that run with a nasty rooster, and he has the peck marks to prove it."

The idea of a knight of the realm gathering eggs amused Lizzy, and she rewarded the gentleman for sharing his tale with a smile.

"When I was a young girl, Longbourn was still a working farm operated by two tenant farmers. I recall acres and acres of wheat, barley, and hops."

"...which were all sold to a brewer."

"Yes. The entire crop went to the Elmwood Brewery in Watford," Lizzy acknowledged. "But because the house is 200 years old, and such an old building requires repairs, we sold all but ten acres of the property to pay for its upkeep."

"I understand perfectly. We have the same difficulties at my home in Derbyshire."

"Yes, I am sure the Darcys of Derbyshire face the same problems as the Bennets of Hertfordshire." But Lizzy did not wait for Mr. Darcy to respond. "We had best move on," she said, swatting at some insects. "Are the night fighters as bad as these gnats?"

"Yes, and they employ the same tactics. Come in at you head on and in great numbers."

Once they were a safe distance from the marauders, Darcy asked Elizabeth to stop.

"There is another reason why I asked you to come out here. I do believe we have met and not just because you look familiar. It is obvious you don't like me. Oh, yes, I did notice," he said, noting her expression, "and although there are people who dislike me, I usually know the reason for their antipathy. So, tell me, have we met?"

Lizzy reddened. She *had* been rude, but that was because Mr. Darcy's remarks at the pub had stung. Although she wasn't as pretty as Jane or Kitty or Lydia, with their blonde hair and blue eyes, she thought she could hold her own, but the man had been more interested in his brew even after Mrs. Corker had declared her to be a local beauty.

"I would not say we have *met*, but we were in each other's company last week at The Hide and Hare."

While he mulled over her statement, Darcy's brow furrowed, but then the light came on. "Ah, the lady in trousers."

"Yes, I was wearing trousers," Lizzy said defensively, "but surely Britain has been at war long enough that a woman in a pair of trousers is not such a rarity."

"A woman who looks *good* in trousers is still a rarity. I can assure you of that."

"I will take that as a compliment."

"Which was how it was meant. But as to my behavior at The Hide and Hare, the only excuse I have is that I was… I was…"

"…pissed." After Darcy's eyes widened, Lizzy chuckled. "You are surprised to hear such a word uttered by a woman who wears trousers and muddy boots?"

"Yes, I was pissed," Darcy said, laughing. "I was

unhappy with my new assignment as an instructor of trainees. After two weeks of doing nothing but taking off and landing, I was feeling sorry for myself, and I got drunk at The Hide and Hare. Now, the only thing left for me to do is to apologize."

"I accept your apology, but I think a penance is in order." Darcy arched his eyebrows. "You must tell me your story about the Hurricat—the one you didn't want to share when we were in the manor house."

Darcy agreed to her condition. "It's not that I object to telling the story over and over again, usually at Bingley's prompting. But from past experience, I shall warn you, the ladies don't find it nearly as amusing as Bingley does."

"May I decide for myself?"

"All right then. You have been warned," and Darcy began his story. "When the war broke out, I signed on with the Royal Air Force with the idea of flying fighter planes and saving the day, so to speak, by shooting down numerous German bombers and fighters in aerial combat over the Channel. But the RAF had other plans for me. Instead of a Spitfire, I was trained on a Hurricane or Hurricat as it was called.

"Before the British Navy had escort carriers to protect transatlantic convoys, there were specially outfitted merchant freighters who catapulted these aging Hurricanes off their decks for the purpose of engaging the German fighters that were harrying British merchant shipping."

"When you say 'engage,' do you mean like the Spitfires did with the German fighters in the Battle of

Britain?"

"Yes and no. Of course, the best result was to shoot them down, but if we couldn't do that, then, at least, we wanted to chase the Germans away from the convoy. Because we could not land on the ship after a sortie, we had to go into the water. Once out of the Hurricat, I would sit in an inflatable dinghy and wait to be picked up. The first few times went off like clockwork, and I was found right away. The next two times were a bit dicier, and I was out there for quite a while. It was on my eighth sortie that my luck ran out. They couldn't find me for the longest time, and when they did, I was seriously dehydrated and suffering from hypothermia."

"How long were you out there?" Lizzy asked, gulping at the idea of someone being given a one-way ticket out over the Atlantic.

"Long enough to become delirious. I had reached the point where I thought it would be a good idea to slip over the side. I have since been told that it is a rather common delusion. Remember, on the Atlantic, there is nothing to mark where you are, and you become disoriented rather quickly."

"You didn't go back into the water, did you?" Lizzy had to agree with Mr. Darcy's female audience. She didn't find much to amuse in this story.

"I was about to when someone told me...," but then he stopped and stared at Lizzy, recalling the first time he had seen her, and it had not been in The Hide and Hare. "Fortunately, I saw a... I saw the searchlight of a ship," he continued. "Once I was back on land, they found I had double pneumonia. It took awhile to shake that off, and then I was assigned to Bomber Command. Actually, I preferred piloting the Hurricat because if something went wrong, it was only my arse in the wringer. Oh, I am sorry."

"Believe me, I have heard a lot worse language in the canteens. Please continue."

But their conversation was interrupted by the sound of bombers flying overhead.

"Right on time," Darcy said, looking at his watch, and then Lizzy followed his gaze as he watched each lonely bomber climb into the late afternoon sky with a destination of the harbor facilities at Le Havre or the railway yards at the Pas de Calais.

"My father keeps track of these things," Lizzy said, interrupting Darcy's thoughts. "He believes most of the missions from Helmsley are to the Low Countries or France in preparation for the invasion."

"Your father would be right. But since I have spotted winged intruders at 10:00, 2:00, and 12:00 high," Darcy said of the circling gnats, "our only choice is evasion. Shall we go in?"

Chapter 5

When Elizabeth and Darcy went into the library, Jane and Charles were nowhere to be found. They soon learned from Mr. Buttons that the couple had gone for a walk in the direction of Meryton.

"Miss Jane said that you need not wait for her," Mr. Buttons told Lizzy.

"Well of all the nerve," Lizzy said, putting her hands on her hips in feigned outrage, but then she smiled to let him know she really wasn't upset.

"Would you like tea or coffee, miss?" Buttons asked. "Take the chill off."

"Oh, how marvelous that you have tea. At Longbourn, we have already used up our tea ration for the month."

"The Americans left the larder full of all kinds of goodies, including tea and biscuits and a delectable confectionary treat called a Twinkie."

"Mr. Buttons, I cannot possibly pass up anything called a Twinkie."

After the butler left, she told Darcy that as soon as she finished her tea, she would get out of his hair.

"You are not in my hair," Darcy said, "so please sit down and tell me why you were in The Hide and Hare wearing trousers."

"I am a lorry driver." Her comment resulted in another furrowed brow from Mr. Darcy, something Lizzy found adorable. "I am a member of the Auxiliary Territorial Service. My main job is to collect fresh fruits and vegetables from farms for the grocers and canteens in the South Midlands, but I have also hauled firewood, tents, and, on occasion, manure. It's amazing how fast you can drive when you have a pile of you know what in the back of your lorry," she said with a chuckle. "But I also take the local girls from the village to the dances on the bases."

"Presumably not in the same lorry as the manure."

"We *usually* wash it out first," Lizzy said, laughing. "Up to this point, I've only taken the girls to the American dances, but there will be a dance at Helmsley this weekend. Considering your low opinion of the local beauties, I imagine you will not be attending."

"Is that what I said in the pub that gave such offense?" Lizzy nodded. "No wonder you didn't want to walk with me in the garden. Again, my apologies. I can assure you it had nothing to do with the village lovelies and everything to do with my injured pride at being given a training assignment. In other words, I was sulking."

"You also inferred that your dance partners at the Netherfield dance had two left feet."

"Now that part was true," he said, smiling.

"But, seriously, you did survive the mission over Nuremburg, or so I was told by the owner of the pub. Surely, that indicates a level of skill the RAF would want their younger pilots to acquire."

Darcy registered surprise that a piece of his biography was known outside the elite group of men who flew the RAF's premier bomber, but he also understood that the Nuremberg raid was so devastating that those who came back were looked upon with something like awe.

"My surviving the Nuremberg mission was entirely a matter of luck. I was in the lead group, and we went through with no difficulty. But the planes coming behind us hit strong headwinds, and they drifted into a group of German fighters who exacted a heavy toll. So skill had nothing to do with it. However, I *am* a skilled dancer."

"Are you saying you *will* attend the dance a week Saturday?"

"That depends. Are you going?"

"Yes, I have to go. It is my job to collect the girls at the church. After I drop them off at the canteen, I help with serving the refreshments or in the kitchen. So I do go to the dances; I just don't dance."

"You don't dance at all? Not even at the Yank bases?" Darcy asked in a surprised voice. "I hear they have the best bands."

"That's true. They have the best of everything and in large quantities."

"Then why don't you dance?"

Lizzy hesitated. There were so many reasons why she didn't participate, but she chose to give the most basic explanation.

"When the Americans first came to Helmsley, I did attend their dances. Everyone in the village was so grateful for their help, and it seemed the right thing to do. And it is true that their bands are very good. Apparently, in America, even the smallest towns have good bands. A sergeant from Tennessee told me that in the American South everyone is born knowing how to play a fiddle or mouth organ or pick a guitar. I'm sure it was an exaggeration, but they do have excellent musicians, especially the drummers."

"If the bands are so good and you like to dance, then why did you stop going?"

Lizzy said nothing, hoping her silence would indicate that she preferred not to answer, but Darcy wasn't letting her off the hook. A reprieve arrived with Mr. Buttons serving the tea and the Twinkie, a yellow cake stuffed with a vanilla filling. The last time Lizzy had tasted cake was nine months earlier when everyone had shared their ration coupons for sugar for a birthday cake for their father's fiftieth birthday, sugar usually being reserved for the family's tea and coffee. After allowing Elizabeth to digest her treat, Darcy pressed her on why she did not go to dances.

"The Americans, especially those from the enlisted ranks, were very young—many barely in their twenties, and they were so far from home. They all seemed to want to find that special girl, and I found myself spending most of my time refusing requests for dates. It's not that I didn't like the Yanks," Lizzy quickly added. "If you have been to North Meryton, you will see the Americans are in all the shops and restaurants, and whenever I am in the village, I always stop and chat and ask them where they are from. As a result, I have met a Yank from thirty-two of the forty-eight states and one from the Alaskan territory."

"I'm sure one of your missing states is Montana. I have been there, and there are more cows than people."

"Why did you go to Montana?" Lizzy asked. She knew exactly where Montana was as there was a map of the United States in her father's study. Whenever she met someone from a particular state or territory, she would stick a red pin in the map. After looking up the state in the atlas, Mr. Bennet had declared

Montana to be a 3M state: mining, mountains, and manure.

"When I was thirteen, I went to a dude ranch in the Rocky Mountains with my mother's brother, Lord Antony Fitzwilliam, the current Earl of Stepton, who, for one month, fancied himself to be a cowboy, that is, a cowboy with a valet and a hamper from Fortnum's."

"What did you do on the dude ranch?" Lizzy asked, laughing at the thought of the Earl of Stepton herding cattle with a manservant in tow.

"Lots of things. I learned to rope a calf and ride a bucking bronco, that is, a horse. You look surprised, but I can actually do those things. Granted, those skills are not in demand in London or Derbyshire, but one never knows what surprises life will serve up as I never imagined myself as being a pilot. I also learned that Americans, or at least those who live in Montana, will put beans in any dish, that they have a plug of tobacco in their cheeks at all times, and can spit great distances because they have lots of practice doing it."

Lizzy was finding this Mr. Darcy much more engaging than the man who had ignored her at The Hide and Hare, and she was quite content to spend an afternoon talking to him. "So you are a native of Derbyshire?"

"Yes, and proudly so." Darcy spent the next ten minutes acquainting Elizabeth with the glories of living on an estate situated so near to some of England's most beautiful landscapes in the Peak District. The manor house, a stone mansion built in the early 18th century, faced west in the direction of White Peak, and according to its occupant, glowed in the afternoon sun. Darcy confessed that he and his sister had enjoyed an idyllic childhood growing up on an estate nestled in rolling countryside and one that was home to centuries-old oaks, horse chestnut trees, and towering pines, with coursing streams partitioning the property. "Have you been to the Peak?"

"Yes, but, unfortunately, the weather was so bad, we couldn't see anything. Out of necessity, we confined our travels to visiting the spa at Matlock."

"You absolutely must go back. In fact, I shall issue an invitation right now for you to visit Pemberley, I mean, once the war is over. Right now, the manor house is being used by His Majesty's Government. I imagine that at this point it is pretty scuffed up. Fortunately, my father keeps an eye on things."

"Is your mother alive?"

"Yes, but she stays at the townhouse in London. It is being used as an officer's club for the duration of the war, and she runs it for the Red Cross. My parents are separated, and although they do get on, it is no hardship for them to live so far apart."

But there was something in the way Mr. Darcy uttered those words that made Lizzy think there *was* hardship, at least for their son.

* * *

"And where have you been?" Jane asked as soon as Lizzy walked in the door at Longbourn.

"Where have *I* been? *You* left me at Netherfield. Thank you very much."

"Charles and I waited and waited. But when you didn't come back, we went for a walk. What did you and Mr. Darcy get up to?"

"Mr. Darcy and I got up to nothing. We walked to the fountain, which is now a gnat-infested, slime-covered puddle, and chatted, and please do not turn this brief encounter into a 'William Darcy and Lizzy Bennet' tale. I do not want my name coupled with anyone for the duration. You know that."

Jane did know that, but she never understood why her sister refused to cultivate friendships with members of the opposite sex. Her answer, "after the war," never satisfied.

"Although my opinion of the gentleman has changed, I learned enough about him to know we have little in common. He is obviously someone from the social elite, so Mr. Darcy would have no interest in the daughter of a local magistrate."

"Yes, he *is* a member of the social elite.

According to Charles, Mr. Darcy is on the short list to inherit the title of Earl of Stepton as the current earl has only one heir and a spare, making him third in line. But why would you think he would have no interest in you?"

"Because someone as handsome as Mr. Darcy will have society girls falling all over him." Lizzy thought about his dark, wavy hair, gorgeous green eyes, and the adorable cleft, and she pictured tracing the outline of his jaw, allowing her finger to rest on the dimple in his chin. "But enough about that gentleman. Tell me about Charles."

"Oh, Lizzy! He is a darling man." Jane shared some of what she had learned from Charles during their afternoon together. The Bingleys were originally from Scarborough, but Charles's grandfather had gone out to South Africa as a young man and had made his fortune there. Like so many from the far reaches of the Empire, the senior Mr. Bingley had sent his children back to England to be educated, and Charles's father had attended Cambridge. After marrying an English girl, the family had settled once again in the north of England.

"Lucky for you the grandfather saw the benefits of a British education," Lizzy said, smiling, but then she became serious. "Jane, do be careful. You were devastated by the news about Jeremy, and Charles is a pilot..."

"You need not say another word. I know how dangerous flying a bomber is. However, at this point, I just want to get to know Charles better, and since he is scheduled to fly a mission for the next four nights that will give me time to think about what would be involved if our friendship should become something more serious. I shall go into this with my eyes wide open."

"That is all I ask."

Chapter 6

After a long day of visiting the farms of Cambridgeshire, Lizzy parked her lorry at the depot in Meryton and ran her gloved hands back and forth along her thighs trying to generate friction and heat. All during the winter months, Lizzy had received promises from Abel Jenner, the chief mechanic, that the heater in her lorry would be repaired. But this evening, when she had again asked about it, she had been told that with the arrival of spring, heaters were no longer a necessity. That was news to Lizzy, especially when she thought about all the mornings she found it necessary to scrape the frost off her windscreen or the evenings when temperatures dropped as quickly as the setting sun.

"If it's so warm out, then why am I still wearing my winter coat and wool-lined boots?" Lizzy asked Abel.

"If you're that cold, go get yourself a cuppa at the canteen," tea being the mechanic's cure for every complaint. "Mrs. Dickens has the kettle boiling for you."

Lizzy's preference would have been to head for Longbourn and a warm bed, but despite being outfitted like an Eskimo, she couldn't shake the chill that had settled in her bones. Walking past the shed where her bicycle was stored, she headed for the canteen.

"Just brewed a fresh pot of tea," Mrs. Dickens said by way of greeting. "And it's a good thing because I can tell you're freezing." When handed the mug, Lizzy wrapped her hands around it, allowing the heat to defrost her frozen digits and nodded her thanks. "Too tired to chat, are ye? Well, that's too bad because that officer's been waiting for you for quite some time now."

After scanning the poorly lit canteen, her eyes rested on a handsome man with wavy black hair, green eyes, and cleft in his chin and that someone was now gesturing for her to join him. As soon as she saw him, the fatigue that had plagued her for the whole of the afternoon evaporated. Mr. Darcy had come calling.

* * *

"Tonight's mission was cancelled. Bad weather over the target," Darcy explained after Elizabeth had deposited her weary frame into a wooden chair across the table from him.

"For your sake, I am happy to hear it," Lizzy answered. "Mrs. Dickens said you've been waiting for me." Darcy nodded. "That's a risky business. I don't often stop in the canteen. I'm usually so tired I head straight for home."

"I made sure that wouldn't happen tonight. I gave the mechanic at the depot a fiver to send you my way."

Lizzy smiled, both pleased and surprised to find Mr. Darcy waiting for her. During their afternoon at Netherfield, she had found that once the gentleman's hard façade was chiseled away, he was excellent company. But after he had walked her home, she had no expectations of seeing him again. He certainly hadn't said anything to indicate otherwise.

"You work long hours."

"Lately, yes," Lizzy acknowledged. "It's all the Yanks on the road moving their equipment to staging areas in the South. It creates quite a bottleneck. Unlike last week, today I was able to weave in and out of all the traffic because they have more military police directing traffic. Snowdrops, they call them, because of their white helmets. How long have you been waiting?"

"Not long. Five, six hours." When Lizzy's mouth fell open, Darcy started to laugh. "Less than an hour. Allowing for distance, road conditions, wind, and weather, I estimated your time of arrival at the canteen to be somewhere between 6:30 and 7:30." Lizzy had no idea if the man was serious, but then he continued. "As part of my training as a pilot, I was required to take a course in navigation."

"But you didn't know where I was coming from," Lizzy said, finally realizing he was having her on. "Admit it. You guessed."

"Found out so easily," he said, looking directly into her eyes. "Do you enjoy driving a lorry?"

For Lizzy, it was better than most of the alternatives for a young woman classified as mobile. She had no illusions as to the hard work required of the Land War girls who worked on the farms or the homesickness experienced by those who were sent to work in factories far from their families nor did she want to be a nurse or nurse's aide serving as a Voluntary Aid Detachment.

"When the war started, I took a first-aid course from the Red Cross," Lizzy explained. "The instructor arranged for us to go into London to participate in a staged emergency, but when we arrived, we found that the previous evening the Germans had bombed a nearby neighborhood. We were immediately put to work helping the victims of the bombing. Although I performed well enough, I knew this was not something I wanted to do on a daily basis. When I was called in for my interview, I told the board I knew how to drive a lorry."

"Did you?"

"When I was still in school, I drove my aunt's delivery van for her florist shop. Although I was stretching the truth a bit, it was good enough to qualify me for the position."

Darcy mentioned that his sister, Georgiana, was serving as a VAD in Italy. "Before the war, I would never have imagined such a thing, but she's bloody good at it." Lizzy could hear the pride in his voice that his sister had accomplished such a thing.

"My Aunt Ruth, who is married to my mother's brother, John Gardiner, was a VAD in The Great War, which is how she met my uncle, but she was originally from Derbyshire, a village called Lambton. Are you familiar with it?"

"Yes, indeed! Lambton is the nearest village to

Pemberley." According to Darcy, for more than a hundred years, Lambton had served as a stop for tourists on their way to the Peak District, but the village had suffered between the wars when a more direct route between Derby and Matlock had been paved, bypassing the village. "Lambton is a place frozen in time. For those who leave the main road, they will find an inn that was built during the reign of George III and several half-timbered shops. It's quite a pretty little village."

"That is exactly how my Aunt Ruth described it. I wonder if your family knew her?" Lizzy asked, doubting it very much.

"I'm sure they did." Lizzy looked skeptical.

Darcy explained that the biggest social event in Lambton was the annual flower show held every August at Pemberley. "Because my mother is the chairwoman, she is a social butterfly flitting about the grounds, shaking hands with adults, patting the heads of their children, and awarding ribbons. During the festivities, she trotted out her own children like two of her prized roses. Everyone would ooh and aah over Georgie with her angelic face and golden ringlets. She was absolutely adorable in her white pinafore and bloomers."

"And you would have been in your plaid cap with the little button on top and a suit with short pants."

"Just so. But no ringlets," Darcy said. "But I can see that you are tired, so I shant keep you much longer. However, I did come with a purpose. It's about the dance on Saturday at Helmsley. If *I* asked you to go, would that change your mind?"

William's request caused Lizzy's heart to flutter, and for a second, she considered breaking her rule not to become involved with any man for the duration of the war. But in the end, her answer would remain "no."

"I'm sorry. It wouldn't change my answer," she said, shaking her head. "Until this blasted war is over, it's best not to... I have so many friends who are in the thick of it or who have been wounded or taken prisoner or they have been..." But then Lizzy went quiet.

"...killed. I've experienced the same thing."

"Of course, you have. I didn't mean to imply..."

"I didn't think you were. Excuse me for being so forward, but did you lose a sweetheart in the war?"

Lizzy shook her head. "No, I did not, but Jane did. Her fiancé was in tanks with General Montgomery and died at El Alamein. With Jeremy's death, I lost one of my dearest friends."

After several moments of an uncomfortable silence, Lizzy changed the subject. "Do you know if the commander at the station has contacted the churches or the local council about arranging for girls to attend the dance? After all, it is the first dance open to the public. Not everyone will know about it."

"I have no idea." Then it occurred to Darcy why Elizabeth would ask such a question. She didn't think anyone would show up—not with the Americans at Nuthampstead having a dance on the same night. "Obviously, that would be a problem for the lads," Darcy said, biting his lip as if this was a matter of great concern. "Actually, if enough ladies don't show up, it could prove to be a real morale killer. Might affect a lad's performance down the line. So I take your point. It is of the greatest importance that *every* young girl do her bit and come to the dance."

"Oh, aren't you clever, Mr. Darcy?" Lizzy said, laughing.

"William. Please."

"As I mentioned earlier, *William*, I *am* going to the dance and will gladly serve you a pint of real ale or a Coca Cola as it is my understanding the Americans left pallets of the soft drink behind at Helmsley. As far as doing my bit, I drive a lorry five days a week, through all kinds of weather, all over the South Midlands. I am already doing my bit."

"You can't blame a bloke for trying," Darcy said. Looking at his dazzling smile, Lizzy felt that flutter again. "But I shall see you on Saturday? Yes?"

"Behind the wheel of my lorry or in the kitchen, but, yes, I shall be there."

Darcy walked Elizabeth to the shed where she stored her bicycle. Despite her rejection concerning the dance, he was not without hope of seeing her again, and so he took her hand in his. When he did, she looked at him with her luminous eyes, two dark orbs he knew he would never forget. Once before, on a coal-black night, she had reached out to him and had saved him. Now it was his turn to return the favor.

Chapter 7

Before dinner, Lizzy shared with Jane her concern that few of the local girls would attend the dance on Saturday night because of competition from the American base. As a result, it would be necessary for her to launch her own recruitment drive, starting with Kitty. Lizzy thought it would be best if Jane asked their younger sister to do the right thing by the British airmen as it was much more difficult to say "no" to dear sweet Jane than to wave off cranky old Lizzy.

"I already told Lizzy I was going to the dance at the American base," Kitty repeated during dinner.

How clever of you, Kitty, Lizzy thought. *You avoided saying 'no' to Jane by saying 'no' to me.*

"Kitty, just this one time. Please?" Lizzy pleaded and then looked to her father. "We need every girl we can get. It's the first dance since the RAF's return, and it has not been properly advertised."

Mr. Bennet did not wait for his younger daughter to respond. "Kitty, you are going to the Helmsley dance or you not going to *any* dance. And don't, 'But,

Papa,' me. It is the first dance open to the public, and it is your duty to make these young flyers feel welcome. Every time you hear a plane overhead, you should understand that those men are risking their lives for *you*, and I can tell you from personal experience that during The Great War a dance was a slice of heaven to my fellow Tommies and me. I will not see these young men sit on the sidelines for want of a partner if there is something I can do about it."

Mrs. Bennet, who was always looking out for her younger daughters, saw an opening. As a young girl, she had liked nothing better than a dance, and she thought it unfair for Mr. Bennet to insist that Lydia must wait until she had finished school before attending her first dance. After all, Lydia was eighteen and would soon be working at the uniform factory. In her mother's opinion that qualified Lydia as an adult, and she should be afforded adult privileges.

"Tom, I agree with you," Mrs. Bennet said. "It *is* our patriotic duty to support our young men in uniform, and because of that, I think Lydia should be allowed to go to the dance—just this one time. Like you said, they need every girl they can get."

Lydia, who had only been half listening, was now all ears. "I think that's an excellent idea, Papa. I would like to do my bit just like my sisters. What do you think?" Lydia's big blue eyes pleaded with her father.

"Dearest Lydia, how generous of you to offer to dance for your country," but the sarcasm was lost on both mother and daughter. "You asked for my opinion, and here it is. If I allow you to go to this dance, I will be opening the door to every other dance held by the British *and* Americans. But if I do not agree, for the next week, I will be hounded and badgered until I give my consent.

"However, some good may come of it. It may mean that you will stop pretending to be at Maria Lucas's house studying for your exams when you are actually walking up and down High Street flirting with the Americans." Lydia's uncomfortable look confirmed her father's statement. "Did you really think I wouldn't find out? As the local magistrate, there is little that does not reach my ears. But because your older sisters will be there to stand up with you, I shall say 'yes' to this one dance."

"Well, if I am ordered to go," Kitty said, "then I shall tell all my friends and convince them to go to the Helmsley dance as well. But on one condition. Lizzy must go. And I do not mean just handing out refreshments. She, too, must dance with the men."

Mr. Bennet was surprised to hear that his daughter did not dance, especially because she often stepped lively in the sitting room when a favorite tune came on the radio or while playing one of her records on the Victrola, and he wondered why she had stopped.

"Yes, I agree. Lizzy must do her part as well, especially since the plea originated with her."

Now all eyes were on Lizzy, and she did not see how she could wiggle out of dancing with the airmen. As her father had said, it had been her idea in the first place.

"I shall go, and I shall dance," Lizzy said as she straightened her skirt, a nervous habit she had when she was put on the spot. When Lizzy looked at Jane, she could tell her older sister already had her dancing with William Darcy. Because Lizzy had been so insistent that she would not dance, she wondered if William would even be there. It was then that she realized how very much she wanted to see him. When he had taken her hand, she felt as if a bolt of electricity had run through her, and she wondered what it would be like to be held in his arms.

* * *

The Bennet sisters were so successful in getting the word out that Lizzy had to make two trips to the church in order to transport all the girls to the Helmsley dance. When Lizzy went into the canteen, she found the hall filled with young men dressed in RAF blue and girls in their Sunday dresses, many of them wearing nylons, gifts from the Americans at Nuthampstead. Looking at the youthful faces of some of the airmen, she realized that at twenty-three she might very well end up dancing with someone who was four years her junior—a rather uncomfortable thought.

As soon as they were inside the canteen, Jane found Charles waiting for her, and in a shot, he was by her side. *They make such a handsome couple,* Lizzy thought. *What beautiful children they will have,* the marriage already a given.

After encouraging the pair to get out on the dance floor, Lizzy gravitated to her usual post and asked the ladies serving the refreshments if they needed any help.

"We weren't expecting such a crowd, so an extra pair of hands would be welcomed, Elizabeth," Mrs. Peters, the organizer, answered. "As my dear mother always said, 'Many hands make light work.'"

Before Lizzy could get her apron on, someone reached out and took hold of her hand. It was Darcy. "There's a rumor going around that you are breaking with your curmudgeon past and that you intend to dance."

"And who started this rumor?" Lizzy asked, believing Jane was responsible.

"I did." When Darcy smiled, she thought she would go weak at the knees and felt like a teenaged Judy Garland singing *You Made Me Love You* to Clark Gable's picture.

"But I told Mrs. Peters I would help in the kitchen," Lizzy said, now regretting that she had volunteered.

"Oh no you don't, Elizabeth Bennet!" Mrs. Peters said. "You didn't tell us you had come to dance. Now, hand me that apron and get out there on the dance floor."

The band was playing Harry James's *Two O'clock Jump*. Because it had been so long since Lizzy had danced, at least in public, she wasn't sure she could pull off the steps, especially with the way the band was playing it.

"Come on, Elizabeth. It's like riding a bicycle," Darcy said, and he was right. The band's next selection was a foxtrot. Because William was such an excellent dancer, they danced across the floor as if they were Fred Astaire and Ginger Rogers.

When the band had finished, they announced that they had a request for the Hokey Pokey, a huge favorite with the crowd as it did not require that one have a dance partner or, for that matter, any ability to dance. Even though she felt perfectly silly putting her backside in and her backside out, Lizzy smiled throughout, especially because William and she were directly opposite to Jane and Charles. When the dance was over, the two couples met in the middle and dissolved into laughter.

The Hokey Pokey was followed by a conga, and everyone formed a line that snaked its way around the canteen. Lizzy was enjoying herself immensely, especially since the noise required that William whisper in her ear when he had anything to say, and it didn't hurt to have his hands resting on her hips. But as soon as the music stopped, Jane and Lizzy were surrounded by young men asking them to dance. Reluctantly, they left their partners. After all, the purpose of their coming to the canteen was to do their bit and that meant dancing with airmen other than William and Charles.

Before Lizzy left for a spin around the dance floor with a young Scot, whose accent was as impenetrable as a Highland fog, Darcy insisted that if the band played *I'll Be Seeing You*, it was his intention to claim the dance, and Charles seconded the idea. While the ladies danced, the men filled out a dance request card for the song. But they would have to wait their turn. Before the band played the requested song, Lizzy and Jane had cheered up a good portion of the Commonwealth. While Jane danced with a British Columbian, an Australian, and a New Zealander, in addition to the Highlander, Lizzy tripped the lights fantastic with natives of Toronto and Johannesburg. Feeling that he had waited long enough, after the dance with the South African had ended, Darcy intercepted Lizzy and quickly ushered her out the back door.

"Is there someplace we can go where I won't have to share you?" Darcy asked.

"I can't leave if that is what you are asking. I'm

the lorry driver," Lizzy reminded Darcy. "I have to take the girls back to the village."

"Oh, damn, I forgot," Darcy answered and lit a cigarette. "But let's stay out here for a bit or I won't have a chance to talk to you."

"All right. But once the band starts playing again, I have to go in as I am committed for at least two dances to Australians who put in specific requests."

"Bingley and I did that ages ago for *I'll Be Seeing You*."

"Oh dear, bad choice. That's always the last song of the evening or at least that was the way it was when the British were first at Helmsley."

"Why didn't you say something when I asked you for that dance?"

"Please don't look at me that way," Lizzy said in response to his furrowed brow. "Remember it was you who told me I needed to do my bit by dancing with the troops and that is what I am doing."

"So the reason you danced with me is because you were obligated to do so? I thought it was because I am irresistible."

"I won't answer that question or you will get a big head," she said, laughing. "Seriously, it *has* been fun. I had forgotten how much I enjoyed dancing." Lizzy thought how stupid she had been to pass up a chance to kick up her heels and enjoy herself during such difficult times. "Kitty and Lydia are certainly having fun."

"Yes, I danced with both of them, and they can really cut a rug. But I see little family resemblance between your three sisters and you."

"I know. It's a family joke. Because my parents both have fair hair and blue eyes, my father insists I was brought to the house by a stork blown off course from one of the Mediterranean countries."

"Lucky for me the stork didn't have navigation aids or I would have had to look for you in Spain or Italy."

Now Lizzy had a quizzical look. "William, you are a puzzle to me. You can be so gracious and generous with your compliments, but you can also be..."

"Rude, abrupt, moody. Guilty as charged," he said, taking a drag on his cigarette. "I know I have a mercurial temperament, and I have a tendency to keep to myself. That's why I wanted to be a fighter pilot. Even though the RAF tried to drown me, I didn't mind flying the Hurricat. With the Lancaster, I am responsible for the lives of six other men. I lost two after the Nuremburg raid, and I have been out of sorts since that time."

"After such a loss, I can understand why you would want to go it alone."

After taking a step towards her, Darcy put his arm around her waist. It was such a tiny waist, but then

Elizabeth was petite—not more than 5'-2". With his arms encircling her, he pulled her close to him and whispered the lyrics to *I'll Be Seeing You*: "…and when the night is new, I'll be looking at the moon, but I'll be seeing you."

While holding her, Darcy thought about the first time he had seen Elizabeth when there had been no moon at all. It was on the night he had ditched his Hurricat in the Atlantic and was very near to freezing to death. In order to stop the shaking that was convulsing his body, he was about to slip over the side of his dinghy when he heard Elizabeth's voice. With his eyes riveted to his celestial visitor, he listened as Elizabeth cautioned him to wait to be rescued—that a ship was nearby. The shivering had immediately ceased, and she had remained with him until the searchlights of the ship had found him.

Darcy considered telling Elizabeth about their first encounter, but thought better of it, as she would think him insane. And it no longer mattered when they first met—being together is what mattered now. After placing his hand on her cheek, Darcy was about to kiss her when he heard the unmistakable accent on an Aussie, and Lizzy stepped away from him.

"Oh, there you are," a lanky Australian said to Lizzy. "The band's about to start up again, and they're going to play *Waltzing Matilda*."

"I'll be right there." Lizzy and Darcy watched the

young man go back into the canteen.

"Damn Aussies," Darcy mumbled. "They're everywhere."

"That's because they are a part of the Commonwealth and are fighting on our behalf. And I did promise the sergeant I would dance with him, and so I must go."

"Yes, but remember, you must save the last dance for me."

Chapter 8

"It must be hard to be so far from home," Lizzy said to Sergeant John McInerney, a flight engineer on a Lancaster bomber and her last commitment of the evening before returning to the arms of William Darcy.

"Even with your lousy weather, I'd rather be here in England than hacking my way through the jungles in New Guinea like a lot of my mates are doing. I can tell you that for sure," the sergeant said in a broad Australian accent. "But I'm not alone. There are about thirty Anzac airmen here, and we found a pub, the Gray Duck, that puts up with our shenanigans."

Lizzy acknowledged that she knew of the pub, a rather seedy establishment in an alley off High Street, but was silent on the reputation New Zealanders and Australians were earning for their prodigious thirst and tendency to settle disputes with their fists.

"Have you been to London?"

"I've been twice, but I'm a country boy from Western Australia. All that cultural stuff is lost on me. I don't really care about dead queens and kings or going to museums. The only reason I went back to London was to find a place where I could get a good steak, but no luck there either. I ate at a Lyons Corner House, and I would have needed a sharp-edged saw to get through the beef they served." The sergeant then realized he had just knocked England's weather, food, and culture. "No offense, ma'am, but I'd give my left arm for a good steak."

"No offense taken, Sergeant. I know exactly how you feel as I haven't had a steak in four years. Because there is nothing to be done about it, we try not to complain. It also reinforces the British stereotype—stiff upper lip and all that."

"You haven't had a steak in four years? Crikey! No wonder everyone around here is so pasty looking. Steak is good for the blood."

"I'm afraid being pasty is a permanent condition. We don't have the benefit of boundless Australian sunshine." After dancing in silence for a few minutes Lizzy asked the sergeant if he had been out on a mission.

"Yes, ma'am. I'm no longer a virgin. Oh, excuse me. It's just an expression my mates use."

"I understand the expression, so I'm not in the least offended. But I do draw the line at foul language and certain other topics," Lizzy quickly added as she thought about some of the things she had heard while passing a group of Americans on High Street. One of them had followed up a wolf's whistle with: "Will you look at the tail on that beaver," and it didn't take a translator to explain the sexual connotation.

"No fear. I took the cure early on. I went to a Catholic school, and I didn't like the taste of the soap the sisters put in my mouth after I let go with a cuss word," McInerney said, smiling. "I've been out four times now, and I reckon it's not something I'm ever going to get used to because those German fighters know what they're doing. I've been told that they used to come at the bombers from the rear and blast away. But now they come at you head on because they want to kill the pilot. You see, if they get the pilot, there's a good chance they've killed the whole crew. Saw it happen on my first mission. The Lanc spiraled down like a corkscrew right into the ground and burst into flames."

"Yes, I understand the perils you face. But this is an opportunity for you to get away from the war for a few hours," Lizzy said. But it was too late. The seed had been planted, and she was now thinking of Messerschmitts and Focke-Wulfs coming straight at William's Lancaster.

"Sorry, ma'am. It's just that I'm a flight engineer, and the engineer sits in a dickey seat next to the pilot, you know one of those collapsible seats. So if the pilot gets it, it's likely I'm a goner as well."

"Yes, I understand."

"Sorry again. I'm a bit on edge and not really good with talking to the ladies, especially one as pretty as you."

"I'm sure you are exaggerating, Sergeant. I hear Australia is filled to overflowing with pretty girls."

"That's true, ma'am. But Australia is a long ways away, and I have to make do with what's here."

"Well, thank you for the dance," Lizzy said, amused by McInerney's backhanded compliment. "Do take care of yourself and get back home safely."

Knowing that the next number was *I'll Be Seeing You*, Lizzy went looking for William. But there was no bounce in her step, as visions of bullet-riddled windscreens and dead pilots now filled her thoughts.

As soon as Darcy's eyes met Elizabeth's, he noticed the change. "Did that Aussie say something rude to you? Do I need to punch him in the nose?"

"No, he was a perfect gentleman."

"Then why do you look as if you want to make a run for the exit?"

"Nothing happened, William," Lizzy insisted while rubbing her arms as if chilled. "You have been waiting all night for the band to play this tune, so let's enjoy the dance."

Lizzy tried to relax in William's arms, but images she had witnessed a year earlier at an American airfield flooded her mind. Once again, she could smell the burning wreckage and saw the bodies littering the ground, and the nausea returned.

"I need a glass of water," Lizzy croaked as if she was being strangled.

"You are as white as a ghost. What you need is a stiff drink."

"I can't have a drink. I have to drive. Please, just water."

Darcy returned with the water, but after accepting the glass, Lizzy refused to look at him. Before turning away, he had seen the look of anguish in her eyes—a look he had seen on the faces of his crew as they watched their mates being removed from a badly damaged bomber, their flight suits saturated with their blood.

"Elizabeth, tell me what's wrong," he said, taking hold of her hand. "I can help." But when Elizabeth remained silent, Darcy felt empathy give way to frustration. "I would ask if I could see you again, but I already know the answer to that question. You would merely repeat what you said at the canteen: 'It's better not to get involved.' Right? 'No dances, no dates, no entanglements?'"

"I did not use those words."

"No, you did not. But as someone who has made a practice of keeping people at arm's length, I recognize the behavior. If you don't get to know people, you can't get hurt when they leave you or die. So you say, 'it's better this way,' and I ask, for whom, Elizabeth? Better for whom?" And then he turned and walked away.

* * *

Lizzy made her way to the stage and asked the band leader to announce that the first lorry for Meryton would be leaving in ten minutes. Before climbing into the back of the lorry on the way to the dance, the names of the girls had been noted on a clipboard. From some of the things Lizzy had witnessed during the dance, she already knew a few of the girls would follow an airman to some secluded spot where nature would take its course. She only hoped it wouldn't result in a bundle of joy nine months down the road as Meryton already had its share of girls who were in a family way.

"Where's William?" Jane asked while standing with Charles near Lizzy's lorry.

"I imagine he is on his way to Netherfield," Lizzy answered as she checked off the names of the girls climbing into the lorry. "Jane, while I'm gone with this first lot, please find Lydia and Kitty. I don't want to have to go looking for them."

"Did something happen between William and you?" Jane asked in a whisper.

"Jane, I have to go." Lizzy climbed into her cab knowing she was two girls short. Hopefully, they would be in the queue with the next group.

When Lizzy returned to the canteen, she was confronted by an angry Lydia. Apparently, Jane had dragged her away from an American, who had snuck into the dance, and she was railing against her sister's interference. On the other hand, Kitty had a look on her face that told Lizzy she had fallen in love once again, and she would stay in love until the next dance when she would find someone else, which, to Lizzy's mind, was how it should be when you were only nineteen.

"May I ride up front with you, Lizzy?" Jane asked. "Once we get home, I'll be subjected to enough giggling from Kitty and Lydia. I don't need to listen to it all the way to Meryton."

"Climb in."

Lizzy knew it would only be a matter of minutes before the subject of William Darcy arose, but Jane cut her estimate in half. As she had done on numerous occasions, Lizzy explained to her sister that she did not want to become involved with any man until after the war had ended.

"I understand what you are saying, Lizzy. But

isn't it a little different with William?"

"In what way?" Lizzy asked as she shifted gears.

"You like him very much."

"Yes, I do. All the more reason not to get involved." When Jane gave her a disappointed look, Lizzy continued. "You above all people should understand why I do not want to have a relationship with anyone, especially someone who flies a bomber."

"Is that really fair to William?"

"Yes, I *am* being selfish, but have you forgotten the heartache you felt when you received the news about Jeremy? Because I haven't. It was I who dried your tears and comforted you. I simply do not want to experience that pain. Is that so difficult to understand?"

"I shall say no more."

Lizzy could hear the catch in her sister's voice. But to say something now would only lead to more discussion about the horrible things that happened in war, and she had no wish to revisit that subject.

Chapter 9

In England, where everyone talked about the weather, few could remember such a glorious May. With the dreariness of winter behind them, everyone was out and about, and the grassy area around the war memorial on Meryton Common found young people flirting, couples enjoying picnics, and children running around the base of the memorial containing the names of the twelve men from Meryton who had died in The Great War. But for those whose focus was on the current war, many were wondering why the invasion had not gone forward. It would have been a perfect time to storm Fortress Europa, but with May entering its final week, there was little doubt the invasion had been pushed into June.

While the ground forces, now bottled up in camps strung across the South of England, waited for the green light, the bombers of the RAF and the American Army Air Corps were pounding away day after day at anything that might prove to be an obstacle to the Allied forces getting onto the beaches. For Darcy and Bingley, the targets discussed in the briefing room were all beginning to have a *déjà vu* quality to them. During the interrogations following a mission, the pilots were starting to sound like broken records.

Because Darcy's group had flown seven missions in seven days, and with the invasion now definitely pushed into June, the exhausted crews were given two days' leave. Darcy had no intention of spending it reading old magazines in the Netherfield library or drowning his sorrows at The Hide and Hare.

"I doubt if you will want to leave the side of the beautiful Miss Jane Bennet," Darcy said to Bingley, "but I am going to London to meet my cousin, Colonel Fitzwilliam. Are you interested?"

"Sorry, Darcy. As good looking as you are, you are not my type. However, Jane Bennet is. But say hello to Richard for me."

Darcy rendezvoused with his cousin at an officer's club in Knightsbridge. Richard, a colonel in the Sixth Airborne Division, had the swagger of a man who routinely jumped out of airplanes—a paratrooper who was prepared to engage in hand-to-hand combat from the moment he hit the ground. But after months of training and no war, Richard was afraid he was at risk of losing his edge, and because of that, *he* was on edge.

"Honest to God, Will, my men are going stir crazy waiting for the curtain to go up. When does this damn show start?"

"I might actually have an answer for you," Darcy said, lowering his voice. "A few of us at Helmsley have befriended the station meteorologist, and he told us that the invasion comes down to a matter of the moon and tides. According to his calculations, we must go on the 5th or 6th of June or it has to be pushed back two weeks. But keep it under your hat or you will have Army Intelligence paying you a visit, and I shall deny everything and leave you to the tribunals."

"Jolly good, Will! That news deserves a drink." Richard summoned the waiter and ordered two whiskeys. "Do you plan to see your mother while you are in town?"

"In Mama's last letter, she wrote that she would be enjoying a long visit with your mother in Scotland. With so many regiments now in camps in the South in preparation for the invasion, the number of officers coming to the townhouse has dropped off considerably. After all she has done on behalf of the Red Cross, making all those finger sandwiches and brewing up all that tea, I'm sure she decided she had earned a holiday."

"I gather from your tone that you have not forgiven her."

"It's not my place to forgive. It's between my parents and is none of my business."

"Will, I know I'm butting in, but your father…"

"I know what you are going to say. My father had numerous affairs and my mother only the one. But my disapproval of adultery extends to both sexes as demonstrated by the first shouting match I had with my father. At the time, I was fifteen, and it concerned a certain Miss Arminster from Chelsea. And I understand it's all a game. As long as everybody plays by the same rules, everything's fine. But you must admit that by asking my father for a divorce, my mother went out of bounds."

Darcy drained his glass and indicated to the waiter that he wanted another. "The whole thing sticks in my craw. Whether it is my father and the Chelsea widow or my mother and Captain Brown, it's wrong, and people can accuse me of having ridiculous middle-class sensibilities, but what my parents did made a mockery of their marriage vows. I can tell you one thing," Darcy said, pointing his glass in Richard's direction, "My wife had better be absolutely crazy in love with me because there's never going to be anyone else. She's stuck with me."

"I'm beginning to think there is more to this than just your mother's infidelity. After all, she ended the affair months ago."

"Yes. There *is* more. I blame Mama for Georgiana being in Italy. I don't think my sister would have volunteered to become a VAD so far from England if my mother wasn't sharing her bed with the captain. Don't you agree?" But before Richard could answer,

Darcy continued, "And now Georgie has written to tell me that she has fallen in love with an Australian. Bloody hell! An Aussie! Australia is at the end of the world. I'll never see her."

"Come on, Will. Last autumn, Georgie was in love with a doctor from Calgary, so I wouldn't be thinking about booking passage to Sydney just yet. But I still say there is more going on here than your mother and Georgie."

"Don't you have a plane to jump out of?" an annoyed Darcy asked.

"Come on, Will. Let's hear it. Is it a lady?"

Darcy stared into his whiskey glass. Did he really want to tell Richard that he had fallen in love with someone in a ridiculously short period of time, but that the lady had shown him the door? Would Richard mock him if he described the petite brunette as having eyes that a man could get lost in or how he wanted to wrap his fingers around her curls or that her smile could light up a room? Good grief! Elizabeth even had dimples. But his cousin would remind him that he had fancied himself in love before. But now that Darcy had experienced the real thing, he knew that every other woman had been merely a flirtation—a passing moment in time or a way of passing time.

"I was chasing a lady who had no wish to be caught. It's that simple."

Darcy told Richard the story of the whole of his

acquaintance with Elizabeth Bennet, the daughter of a magistrate and lorry driver. "Not much to hold on to, is there? A walk in the gardens. A conversation in a canteen. A dance in a crowded hall. That is the sum total of our time together," he answered, omitting all references to their rendezvous in an inflatable dinghy. Richard would have had a field day with that one.

The colonel was surprised by Darcy's confession. Since his miraculous rescue from the dark waters of the Atlantic, his cousin had played the field, and every one of his amours had been tall, leggy blondes, unburdened by the moral scruples one would find in a village such as Meryton.

"A lorry driver. Now that's interesting."

"If Princess Elizabeth can be a mechanic, I think Elizabeth Bennet can drive a lorry," Darcy said defensively.

"I meant that she sounds very middle class—not exactly your type of girl. Does she have legs that go on for miles?"

"You mean, like Amanda Selridge?" a beautiful lady, but one with a heart of stone. "I hear she eats her lovers after she's finished with them because they seem to disappear."

"That's true," Richard acknowledged. "Amanda is now known as the Black Widow because her lovers tend to get killed as soon as she cuts them loose— even the ones who are not in the military. Did you hear about Adam Bangor? Got pissed, stumbled on a rock, landed in a fountain, and drowned in a foot of water? I wouldn't want that in my obituary. But I was actually thinking of Prissy Cantwell."

"When I was last in town, I rang Prissy's flat, and her flat mate said she wasn't in. So I rang the next day, and I was again told that Prissy wasn't in. I asked if I called every hour on the hour for the next week if I would find Prissy in, and I was told, 'not likely.' It turns out that she threw me over for Lord Corman's son."

"I hear she's very flexible," Richard said with a smirk. "I know she took ballet classes with my sisters. Apparently, all that stretching at the barre paid off."

Darcy refused the bait. He never discussed his liaisons and tuned out those who did.

"I'm sure I got the boot because the Darcys lack a title, and the Cantwells are all about precedence. But you know how it is, Richard. We Darcys disdain titles and rest on our ancient Norman laurels."

"Good for you, Will, you sanctimonious prig. I, on other hand, have no problem with being the son of an earl. In fact, I broadcast it. When I was Canada, it was amazing the mileage I got out of it merely by mentioning that my father was the Earl of Stepton. Opened all sorts of doors for me, and I'm not even the heir. I highly recommend it."

After finishing his drink, Darcy stood up. "Let's

get out of here and find a pub. I feel like getting pissed."

"But no fights, Will. My commanding officer would not be amused if I had to be bailed out of jail just days before the invasion."

"No fights. I promise. I'm already on the schedule for Tuesday."

Chapter 10

Mr. Bennet's prediction that allowing Lydia to attend one dance would throw open the door to other things proved to be accurate. A few days after the dance at Helmsley, the Bennets were entertaining an American, George Wickham—the same Yank who had snuck into the dance at the canteen. Both Lizzy and Jane suspected that their coming together at Helmsley had been no chance encounter, but with ham and butter on the table, courtesy of Corporal Wickham, no one gave voice to their doubts.

Mr. Bennet found himself hugely entertained by the American. Although Wickham was a waist gunner, it seemed there was no position on a Flying Fortress that he was not prepared to man in a crisis, including that of the pilot, and an amused Tom Bennet encouraged him to share his daring escapades on a B-17 bomber.

Charles Bingley, who was also paying a visit to Longbourn, listened as his fellow aviator spun one harrowing tale after another. Although he understood that challenging Wickham would diminish his entertainment value for Mr. Bennet, at one point, the gunner had stretched the truth to the breaking point.

"You took over for the pilot? Was the co-pilot injured as well?"

"You misunderstood me," Wickham answered. "The co-pilot took over for the injured pilot, and I took the second seat. Between the two of us, we got the Fort back to base."

"Admirable," Bingley answered in a monotone because he knew that if anyone would have taken the second seat, it would most likely have been the engineer who was closest to the flight deck. There was also the matter of a waist gunner leaving his position, thus exposing one side of the plane to attack by German fighters. But Wickham certainly wouldn't be the first airman to tell a tall tale. If everyone in the RAF who had ever embellished a story stopped flying, the planes would be empty.

"George is from Hollywood, California," an adoring Lydia said. "He has appeared as an extra in a lot of films."

"Really?" Lizzy asked while looking at her father who was chuckling behind his napkin. "Corporal Wickham, you will find the Bennet sisters are avid cinema goers, and so we are thrilled to have someone from the film capital of the world dining with us. What films were you in?"

"You probably didn't see them. They were mostly oaters. That's what we call Westerns," Wickham explained.

"Perhaps, my father has seen one of your films," Lizzy said. "His favorite movie is *Stagecoach*."

"Yes, but that film being my favorite had more to do with Claire Trevor than John Wayne or any stagecoach," Mr. Bennet answered before winking at Mrs. Bennet.

"No, I was never in a movie with the big stars—those on the A list, I mean. These were all B movies starring Hopalong Cassidy."

"Ah, I see. So you ride. Or is that not unusual in California?" Lizzy asked, continuing to probe.

Wickham explained that California was the second largest state in the United States—only Texas was bigger—and it had every kind of climate and topography imaginable.

"Because the movie biz is such a big employer in Southern California, people learn skills that will get them hired by one of the studios. Being able to ride a horse is a big plus because Hollywood really cranks out the westerns or at least they did before I was dra... before I enlisted."

"And I'm sure it helps that you are so good looking," Lydia said with a sigh.

Both Lizzy and Jane coughed to let their sister know her statement was improper, but the youngest Bennet did not hear them. She was too busy gazing into the corporal's eyes.

After tea, the party adjourned to the sitting room where Jane entertained the family with a tune on the piano. While Jane played, Charles chatted quietly with Lizzy and asked her if she would be attending the dance at Helmsley on Saturday.

"Yes, but in my usual role. I will be collecting the girls at the church and taking them to the dance in the lorry."

"You are not going to dance?" Lizzy shook her head. "Well, I'm sure Darcy will be disappointed."

"No. He already knows of my decision."

"Oh, I see. Maybe that's the reason he slipped off to London."

"Are you learning anything about the differences between British and American bombers from Corporal Wickham?" Lizzy asked, evading Charles's comments about William.

"Not really. I've actually been on a B-17, and although I would compare my gunners with the best of them, I must say that Corporal Wickham is truly exceptional—shooting down two Messerschmitts on one mission—that's really remarkable. The man has performed such feats of daring-do that I can just picture him climbing out on a wing and manually starting an engine whilst in flight." Bingley started to laugh, but then stopped. "That was unkind. Sorry."

"He's obviously trying to impress Lydia, but he need not try so hard as it requires so little effort."

"He's a handsome bloke. I'll give him that. And let's face it. It takes guts to fly missions over Germany, and the waist gunner's position has the highest casualty rate on the Fortresses. He may exaggerate the stories, but the Yanks take it to the Nazis every day and in broad daylight. You have to respect that."

"I do. And I most definitely appreciate his being here in England, especially since he comes with ham."

* * *

After kissing her mother good night, Lizzy was preparing to go upstairs to her room when Mr. Bennet gestured for his daughter to follow him into his study.

"Is something wrong?" Lizzy asked. Usually when someone gained entrance to Mr. Bennet's inner sanctum, there was a serious matter to be discussed.

"Do you mean other than my youngest daughter making a fool of herself over that young American or my wife encouraging it?"

"Mama has always been enthusiastic when it comes to courtships." And this time was no different. She laughed too loud, praised too much, and talked incessantly, all signs of a mother worried about having five unmarried daughters.

Mr. Bennet nodded in agreement. "Despite my concerns for Lydia, this is not about your dear mother or sister, but you. While we were entertaining Corporal Wickham, I overhead you telling Bingley that you do not intend to dance at Helmsley this weekend." Her father wanted to know why.

"I only agreed to that one dance... To get things going... To make sure there were sufficient dance partners for the first dance," Lizzy stuttered, "and believe me there were."

"I'm sorry, Lizzy. It will not do. You are a beautiful twenty-three-year-old girl, and yet you have chosen to stand on the perimeter watching while others enjoy themselves. There must be a reason why you don't dance. Did you have feelings for someone I do not know about? Did you have a sweetheart?"

"No, I swear I did not. It's just something that I..."

"Something that you what? Something you saw?"

Lizzy closed her eyes, tears immediately forming. Other than her trainer, who had been with her on that awful day, she had never spoken to anyone of what she had seen. She did not know how to put into words the sights and smells coming from the wreckage of two B-17s that had collided in the skies above the American base at Basingbourn, and she shook her head. "I cannot speak of it, especially to you."

"You are referring to my time in the trenches. Yes?" Lizzy nodded. "Dear child, it is true I saw many horrific things, but because of that, I don't think there is anything you could tell me that I have not witnessed myself."

Lizzy knew that in the years following the armistice, her father had suffered from nightmares, and he had once declared that only his wife's love and the birth of his children had prevented him from running mad. Lizzy did not want to be the cause of a return of those dreadful memories. But her father, who recognized the look of someone who was carrying a terrible secret, would not let it rest.

"Possibly, it will help you to know that when the memories of those years in the trenches overwhelmed me, I sought out my fellow survivors, a group that included your Uncle John Gardiner. With these men, I shared my experiences from the trenches, and over time, I was able to come to grips with what I had seen and done in France. Talking is not a cure, but it does help."

After wiping her eyes with her father's handkerchief, Lizzy tried to compose herself so that she might share with her father the worst day of her life.

"It happened shortly after the Americans took over Bassingbourn near Royston from the RAF. I was in the lorry with my trainer. After stopping for a cup of coffee, we had just started down the road when we heard a tremendous roar followed by a thunderball coming out of the clouds. Vera pulled over, and we ran in the direction of the sound of the explosion, naïvely thinking we might be of assistance. But all we saw were pieces of metal spiraling through the air and then a body falling into a field, making the most sickening thud when he hit the ground.

"Vera and I thought we might help him, but as we ran toward him, we saw another man in a tree with his face blackened and his arm... Well, it wasn't there anymore. But then we were chased away by the Americans because pieces of the plane were still coming down. We asked what we could do, and one of them said, 'Nothing. You can't do anything. Two planes collided during assembly. They're all dead. All twenty of them,' and then he broke down crying. We tried to comfort him, but he was inconsolable. After the ambulances arrived, we left, but not before I went into the bushes and vomited."

Mr. Bennet put his arm around his daughter's shoulders and encouraged her to continue. No matter how painful, it was best to get such terrible thoughts out in the open.

"A few days after the collision, the base had a memorial service, and Vera and I went. All in a row were pictures of the men who had been killed. I recognized a few of them from the pub in Royston where we would occasionally stop for a meal. There was one man with whom I had danced at the first dance after Bassingbourn had opened. There was no mistaking him as he had red hair and freckles, and he looked to be about sixteen. His name was Patrick Faherty, and he was from Dearborn, Michigan, the home of Ford Motor Company. He told me that when the war was over he was going home to work on the assembly line making sedans just like his dad, and when he had saved up enough money, he was going to buy a convertible and take his girl out for a Sunday drive."

Although tears were racing down her cheeks, Lizzy continued because she really did want to get it off her chest. "I feel such a coward because these men go into harm's way every day, and during the Blitz and the bombing raids, people in the cities suffered terribly and endured so much. I only experienced this one awful day, but it was enough for me to know I don't want to lose anyone. It's bad enough when you barely know them. I don't want to fall in love with someone who is going to climb into a bomber. I read the newspapers. I know all about the Nuremburg raid and the loss of 600 men. Is it so difficult to understand why I don't want to become involved?"

Mr. Bennet took his daughter in his arms and rocked her as if she were his little girl again. "Of course, I understand how you feel because I understand war. But it is not just an army or navy or air force that goes to war. It is a nation. And there are so many ways to bring a nation to its knees, and one of them is to make people afraid. Keep them huddled in their homes unwilling to step outside the door lest they be harmed in some way. That's why cities are bombed—to terrorize the civilian population until the thought of surrender becomes thinkable. The Germans do it to us, and we do it to them.

"But don't you see, Lizzy, if you shut yourself away, the Germans have claimed another victory, and it is a series of small victories that in the end wins wars." And he looked into her eyes when he said that. "You must understand that even if the invasion of France is an unqualified success that the end is nowhere in sight. After we defeat Germany, we still have to fight the Japanese. This could go on for years."

"Oh, Papa, please do not say that!"

"I have to say it because it is true. Hitler and his henchmen are quite willing to fight to the last German and the same with the Japanese. Is it your intention to hide away for another few years? Because if that is your plan, Hitler and Tojo can claim another casualty. Please think about it, Lizzy, because I know you are braver than that."

Chapter 11

Darcy went into Colonel Waterhouse's office. While waiting for the officer in charge of combat operations, he wondered why he had been summoned. He was working his way through a number of scenarios when his CO came in, and he jumped to attention.

"As you were, Flight Lieutenant Darcy." After occupying his leather chair, Waterhouse got right to it. "I know you are still steamed up about the Nuremburg raid."

"Sir, I have said nothing."

"I know you haven't, but if you had, I know exactly what you would have said: 'Full moon. No cloud cover going in. Dodging 88 artillery shells over the Ruhr. No warning about the autocannons.'"

Darcy was stunned that the use of cannons mounted on the top of German night fighters was known to Bomber Command but had not been shared at the mission briefing. "We didn't even know the fighters were beneath us until they fired into our bellies."

"Unfortunately, we had no hard proof about the autocannons until the Nuremburg raid. But in the end, their existence would not have changed the mission. Between you, me, and the lamppost, it was a bloody stupid plan. But Bomber Harris thought differently. He picked the target because Nuremberg was the birthplace of the Nazi party and the site for their jackbooted demonstrations, and it remained largely intact."

"We flew 1,500 miles into the heart of Germany because Nuremburg was a symbol?" Darcy thought he would be ill.

"Of course not. It was a legitimate target with an aluminum works, marshalling yards, and an SS barracks, but that's not why I have asked you here," he said, indicating that the conversation on Nuremburg had concluded. "Because of the success of the Allied bombing campaign, the Nazis have scattered their industry all over Germany and occupied France. As a result, the targets are smaller and harder to find, but because of intelligence from the French Resistance, we can now go after them. However, there is a problem. On the Nuremburg mission, I lost a lot of good men, many of them Pathfinders."

Once Darcy heard the word "Pathfinder," his interest piqued. It was the Pathfinder's job to drop target indicators to light up the aiming point for the bombers. The planes were lightning fast and the positions coveted.

"I can see you are salivating at the thought of getting behind the controls of a Pathfinder bomber. If you can't be a fighter pilot, it's the Mosquito you want because it can outrun anything the Luftwaffe can put up. But I'm not talking about a seven-man bomber," the colonel explained, "but the two-man planes: pilot and engineer. They are the ones who can go after the smaller targets, often flying just above the roofs or treetops.

This was even better, Darcy thought, practically licking his lips. "Jolly good."

"Before signing on, I want to remind you of the downside of flying a Mosquito. The reason it is so fast is because it is made of wood, and if anything hits you, you're very likely a dead man and so is your flight engineer. But if you are up for this, you will have only one other man to worry about. And Mickey Edwards, your flight engineer from Moreston, has already signed on."

"When do I start?"

"If all goes well with the invasion, we are anticipating that we will be able to start the training program sometime in late June in Scotland." Darcy, who was ignoring all the caveats, nodded his head enthusiastically. "Darcy, this is an all-volunteer force, so if there is anything I should know, tell me now. Family difficulties? A girlfriend in London?"

Darcy thought about Elizabeth Bennet's dark

eyes, kissable lips, and delectable wit, but he also remembered the look of resolution on her face when she had told him there would be no more dances, and he shook his head. "No, sir. There's no one."

* * *

"Sorry things didn't work out with you and Elizabeth Bennet," Bingley said as soon as Darcy was back at Netherfield.

"It's just as well," Darcy answered while glancing over his shoulder to see if anyone was listening.

"Why? What's going on?" Darcy acquainted Bingley with his new assignment. "Damn! A Mosquito. I heard it was a Mosquito that hit the Gestapo headquarters in The Hague. Bloody good piece of flying."

"I was probably picked because I have solo experience with the Hurricats." Darcy said, trying to avoid hurt feelings.

"Listen, old boy, you don't have to make excuses as to why you were chosen and not me. You are a damn fine pilot, and the RAF knows it. Besides, I'm not sure I would even want the assignment. Still no armament on the Mosquito?"

"No, it's all about speed. Get in and get out."

"Reminds me of when you were dating Prissy Cantwell."

Chapter 12

"Lizzy, I am so glad you have decided to go to the dance *to dance*," Jane said as she brushed her sister's thick curls. "Does this have anything to do with William?"

Lizzy admitted that it did. There was another reason. After her talk with her father in his study, she decided that she did not want to hide from life; she *did* want to be brave. "If William is still interested in seeing me, then I am all for it. But after what I said to him, I am not sure he will even be at the dance."

"But if he doesn't come, we can let Charles know you are interested in William, and he can talk to him."

Although uncomfortable with the idea of someone working behind the scenes on her behalf, Lizzy agreed to Jane's plan. But there was no time for further discussion as she was scheduled to drive the local girls to the dance.

"Hopefully, we will have a good turnout tonight," Lizzy said as she took one last look in the mirror, and then blotted her lipstick. *Too red*, she thought. *I look like I just took a punch to the mouth.* "Are you going with me to the depot or should I collect you at the church?"

The matter was decided when Lizzy heard the sound of a horn. Her ride to the depot was idling out front.

"Lucinda's early," Lizzy said, glancing at her watch. "I've got to go, so I'll see you at the church." Looking at the pile of dresses on the bed, she added, "You do know that you don't have to fuss so much. You have already caught Charles."

"Yes, I do know I have caught Charles, but there's no reason not to make sure the hook is in good and tight."

* * *

With competition from a dance at the American base, Lizzy knew there would be a drop in the number of girls queuing up for a ride to Helmsley. Even so, when Lizzy saw the crowd, she was pleased. It would be a tight squeeze, but if some of the girls would agree to stand up, she would only have to make the one trip.

After parking the lorry behind the canteen, Lizzy went in to the dance with her fingers crossed, but one look at Jane told her William was not there.

"I really didn't think William would be here," Lizzy whispered to her sister and then greeted Charles who apologized for his friend's absence. "No apology necessary. William never said he was coming. I believe you mentioned he went up to London."

"Yes, he did, and it's his loss that he's not here. May I have the first dance, Elizabeth?" Charles asked.

"Thank you, but, no, you may not," Lizzy answered. "You have been waiting all week to dance with Jane, so please do so. I rather doubt I shall want for partners."

The dance was once again a gathering of Commonwealth forces, thus making conversation easy for Lizzy. She was genuinely curious about where these young men came from and the lives and family they had left behind. Her Australian sergeant from the previous dance found her, but, fortunately, he did not mention any stories involving exploding planes and dead pilots. Instead, she was treated to life on a cattle ranch where steak and eggs was common fare for breakfast. The band wasn't half bad, and Lizzy thought they might actually be practicing— together. As the evening drew to a close, everyone was waiting for that old favorite, *I'll Be Seeing You*, but instead of the song, a colonel stepped up to the microphone.

"Ladies and Gentlemen, please excuse the interruption. I am Squadron Commander Alton of Bomber Command. I hope you have all had a good time tonight as that was certainly our intention." The crowd broke into enthusiastic applause, but when it died down, it was replaced by a palpable tension. Nothing good could come of a senior officer putting in an appearance at a dance. "It is my duty to tell you that all airmen will be confined to the station until further notice and that will be the end of the dances, at least for a while." This statement was met with groans from the military and gasps from the civilians, mostly young girls who had developed crushes on the airmen. "In order to win this war, we have all been assigned jobs, and the time has come for us to do them. But when the battle is won, like the song says, there will be love and laughter and peace ever after and dances as well. Now I shall turn the microphone over to the band leader."

As soon as the major was out of the room, the grumbling began, but the bellyaching was silenced when the band began to play *I'll Be Seeing You*. With the knowledge that the invasion was imminent, the couples clung to each other as it might very well be the last dance for many of them. For Lizzy, because it was now a song that was forever connected to William, she could hardly bear to hear it without him holding her in his arms, and she stepped outside and waited for her passengers by the lorry.

* * *

While the girls found places on the wooden seats of the lorry, Charles, now wearing a long face, waited with Jane. With the announcement that the men would be confined to the station, Lizzy had been expecting to lose a few of her riders, but not quite so many. After ten minutes, she turned on the motor five girls short.

After returning the lorry to the depot, Lucinda drove Lizzy to Longbourn. Although she was tired from a day that had begun at 5:30, she knew the numbing bliss of a deep sleep was not in her immediate future as Jane would want to talk about Commander Alton's order. When she entered Jane's bedroom, Lizzy found her sister lying across her bed crying, and there was little she could say that would comfort her.

"Why did they even bother to have dances at Helmsley if they were only going to have just the two?" Jane asked, sniffling.

"I imagine it was to keep up morale and to take people's minds off the upcoming invasion."

"Now that there are to be no more dances, what about William and you?"

"What do you mean 'What about William and me?'" Lizzy asked surprised. "There is no 'William and me.' I had my chance, but I pushed him away. Now it's too late to do anything about it."

"Don't you dare say it is too late, Lizzy Bennet," Jane said, sitting up and glowering at her sister. "When you are in love, it is never too late. And don't tell me you are not in love. I saw such a change come over you when you were with William that it would be obvious even to a half wit that you have feelings for him." But then her tone softened. "I know you have been trying so hard not to fall in love so as not to risk a broken heart, but I want you to know that even though I was heartbroken when I received the news about Jeremy, I am not sorry I fell in love with him. If something terrible happened to Charles, I will be equally devastated, but that will only make the time we had together all the more precious."

"But what is to be done?" Lizzy asked. "William thinks I want no part of him."

"You can try to ring him at Netherfield, and if telephone calls are not permitted, then you must write to him."

"Write to him? But what would I say?"

"There's nothing easier. Tell him what is in your heart."

Chapter 13

"I can't do this," Lizzy said to Jane as she glanced at the bunched up pieces of paper scattered about her desk. "Actually, I *shouldn't* be doing this. You *do* know that paper is rationed."

"You can make up all the excuses you want, but you are not getting out of this," Jane said, pointing to the paper.

After retrieving a discarded note and smoothing it out, Jane read her sister's first attempt. After balling it up and tossing it into the waste bin, Jane read another, equally bad, missive.

"Lizzy, have you never written a love letter?"

"And to whom would I have written it? I am not the golden-haired Jane Bennet with boys following me around Meryton."

"Well, you can't send these. They're terrible." Jane was about to offer suggestions when, through the door, the muffled sound of their mother's voice could be heard.

"Netherfield Park on the telephone, Jane. I wonder who it can be?" Mrs. Bennet said, her voice nearly a song.

Jane hurried down the stairs and tapped her foot impatiently while Mrs. Ingress, the local exchange operator, asked about the dance on Saturday at Helmsley. She wanted to know if were true that the airmen had been confined to the station.

After the war, Jane hoped the Bennets would have their own telephone line so that they would not have to go through the exchange, thus circumventing the nosey Mrs. Ingress, but she doubted it. Her father, who spent so much of his day at the office on the phone, failed to understand that talking on the telephone could be a pleasurable experience.

"If you need additional information, Mrs. Ingress, you should ring Commander Alton at Helmsley."

"Oh my! I don't want to bother Commander Alton. Please hold for Mr. Bingley."

After a brief conversation, Jane turned around to find her mother standing inches from her. Unembarrassed by her eavesdropping, she repeated her daughter's conversation with Charles.

"It really is too bad that Mr. Bingley is scheduled to fly missions for the next three days. Has he no idea when he will be able to see you again?"

"Shall I ring him back, Mum, so you may speak to him?"

"Don't be cheeky, dear. I'm here to help," she said, patting Jane's arm. "Just make sure you write to him every day so that when he returns, he will have a pile of love letters waiting for him. That's what I did with your father, and I got him, now didn't I?"

After returning to her bedroom, Jane gave Lizzy the bad news. "Charles is on the schedule to fly the next three days, which means I won't see him until Thursday or Friday, and that is only if the invasion doesn't start," Jane mused. "That just won't do."

Lizzy laughed at her sister's comment. Poor Jane! The war was getting in the way of her romance.

"You heard Commander Alton's announcement. Charles is confined to the station."

"Yes, it is true that Charles cannot *leave* Netherfield, but nothing was said about visitors going *to* Netherfield. They are different things entirely."

"Am I speaking to the same Jane Bennet who would not go alone to meet Charles Bingley for tea?"

"Oh, I'm not going alone. You're coming with me."

* * *

Charles and Jane arranged to meet on a service road running behind Netherfield Park, a reminder of the manor's glory days when vans and wagons pulled up behind the house delivering flowers and food for a planned gala. Because Jane's behavior was so out of character, if Lizzy hadn't been a wreck about being arrested by the military police for trespassing, she would actually be enjoying herself.

In an attempt to give the couple some privacy, Lizzy was standing with her back to the lovebirds when she felt a hand on her shoulder, and a vision of the Bennet sisters, clapped in irons in a cold cell, flashed before her.

"You are under arrest for trespassing on military property," a deep voice said. Lizzy felt her heart drop into her stomach; she really *was* going to be arrested.

But when she turned around, she found William Darcy standing there.

"That is not funny, William," Lizzy said, her voice cracking. "You gave me such a fright."

"Serves you right for wandering about Netherfield in the dark of night," he said clearly amused. "By the way, what *are* you doing out here alone in the dark?"

"I am not alone; I am with Jane." She looked around for her missing sister, but Charles and Jane had wandered off. "Wait a minute. What are *you* doing out here?"

"Charles had a telephone call from his sister Caroline, a most persistent lady. Knowing that she will call back and want to talk to me, I decided to find out what he had got up to. And look what I found!"

"From your tone, it sounds as if you came out here bent on mischief."

"Guilty! It's the fun part of being a member of a band of brothers, that is, making life uncomfortable for your mates, and you never know whom you might encounter." Then he smiled, and it was enough to get Lizzy's heart fluttering, and she decided to dive right in.

"William, about the other night at the dance, I am really sorry for the way it ended. I must have seemed incredibly rude to you."

"No, you weren't rude. Unlike some people, I do not confuse honesty with rudeness."

"Thank you for that." Having never been in such an uncomfortable situation, Lizzy was silent, not knowing how to proceed.

"Elizabeth, is there something you want to say to me?"

After hemming and hawing, she finally said what was on her mind. "I know with the invasion and everything that you will be terribly busy, but after things settle down, if you are still…"

"Still what?" Darcy asked eagerly.

"…interested in…"

"Elizabeth, I am not a dentist. I do not pull teeth. What are you trying to say?"

"I was hoping you would still want to see me."

"Damn!"

Lizzy blanched. "Thank you for your honesty, and when you see Jane, please do tell her I have gone home." A mortified Elizabeth quickly walked away, but in a few long strides, Darcy was beside her.

"Why do you want to see me?" Darcy asked, taking hold of Lizzy's shoulders.

With William's touch, Lizzy felt the heat rising in her cheeks. She had experienced a similar response when they had danced together in the canteen with her pulse quickening and a pleasant sensation coursing through her body.

"Because I like you very much."

"Then why did you push me away at the dance?" he asked, inching closer to her. "Something frightened you. What was it?"

This time Lizzy did not hesitate. "Last year when I was driving my lorry past an American airfield near Cambridge…," but she found she could not continue. As a pilot, the gruesome details of a plane crash would not be news to William, but they would resurrect the most horrific memories for her. "Except to say it was the worst thing I ever saw, I would rather not go into details. But because of this horrible event, I thought it would be easier if I didn't become involved with someone I…"

"Yes."

"…with someone I care about."

Darcy took her in his arms and held her against his heart, but then he stopped and stepped away from her. "Your timing is terrible, Elizabeth. In fact, it couldn't be worse."

"I know it is, but I *did* try to see you sooner." She explained how she had gone to the dance hoping he would be there. After Commander Alton had made the announcement that the men were confined to the station, she knew she had made a huge mistake. "I tried to write a letter, but I was unable to put on paper what I was feeling."

"And what are you feeling?" Lizzy said nothing. "Why do you hesitate? Is it because it is always the man who is the first to declare his love?"

Lizzy, who was quick to anger over issues of gender, heard only the insult. "What tosh! I drive a lorry, and I can perform simple repairs on it if necessary. I am an independent woman who…" But then she looked into his beautiful green eyes and asked, "What did you say?"

"I asked if you were expecting me to be the first to declare my love."

"You love me?"

"Isn't it obvious?"

Lizzy flung herself at him and told him that she felt exactly the same way, and then Darcy could not hold back his need to kiss this beautiful woman until her toes curled. From the time he had walked with her in Netherfield's gardens, he had wanted to do that very thing. Finally, Elizabeth Bennet was in his arms, and he kissed her, tasting her mouth, and separating her lips with his tongue. After backing her up to a tree, he moved against her. But the bulk of their coats was interfering with what he wanted to do. He was fumbling with her buttons when he stopped. The previous night he had nearly tripped over a couple in the gardens going at it like two hounds in heat. He knew he couldn't take Elizabeth in that way.

"It's not just the invasion and all that goes with it that will keep us apart," Darcy said, trying to regulate his breathing. "Another assignment has come up that requires additional training in Scotland, and I will be gone for several weeks."

"Scotland? Oh dear, that is so very far. That could be a problem."

To stop her from saying anything more, Darcy kissed her again. "You really would make a terrible pilot, Elizabeth. You think too much," he said, brushing the hair from her face. "When you are flying, you act on instinct. It is the same thing when you are in love."

"I didn't mean to imply it would be a problem for *me*."

"Elizabeth, you would do me a great wrong if you underestimated my feelings for you," he said in a stern voice, but then softened immediately. "For my part, the only difficulty I foresee is dealing with the overwhelming feelings I have for you. Frankly, I haven't been this disoriented since they fished me out of the Atlantic."

"Are you comparing your love for me to being addled in the brain?"

"I am comparing my being in love to the best feeling on earth. But damn it! I won't see you for God only knows how long. It's really a shame. We could have got in an awful lot of kissing if you hadn't been so stubborn."

"Then it is probably for the best that we didn't have more time," she said with a laugh. "Kissing leads to other things."

"Like dancing?" Darcy took Elizabeth in his arms and sang *I'll Be Seeing You* to her. "This is our song, Elizabeth. Whenever you hear it, please think of me."

Chapter 14

Mr. Bennet moved closer to the radio. Two hours earlier, the BBC had confirmed reports that the invasion had begun and that Allied troops had come ashore on the beaches of Normandy.

"Normandy! Not the Pas de Calais as everyone thought," Mr. Bennet said. "Francine, girls, to my study!" he said as if leading a charge. "I have a map of Europe in there."

Throughout the day, as the news trickled in about the invasion, Mr. Bennet moved different colored pins around, puncturing his map of France to indicate where the British, Canadian, and American beachheads had been established. Early news indicated the British and Canadians had moved inland from Gold, Juno, and Sword, those beaches farthest east of Cherbourg. The Yanks on Utah beach were also on the move, but there was still fierce fighting for the Americans who came ashore on Omaha Beach.

"The Yank Rangers had to climb Pointe du Hoc,"

Mr. Bennet said, tapping the map with his finger. "I am familiar with the area as I was in a hospital near Vierville for a week during the first war. The Americans drew the short straw on that one as the beaches are hemmed in by formidable cliffs."

Jane and Lizzy did not have to ask if the squadrons stationed at Helmsley were still attacking targets in France because they could hear the roar of the planes as they flew overhead every day, all day. With air supremacy established, the RAF was now flying daylight raids, something they had not done since 1941.

It wasn't until June 16th, nine days after the invasion, that Charles was able to telephone Longbourn to speak with Jane. "Is it possible for you and Elizabeth to come to Netherfield Park on the evening of the 17th?" Jane's answer was an automatic "yes," but not so with Lizzy.

"I can't go. I am scheduled to drive on the 17th." For ten days, she had been sick with worry, and now that she knew William was safe and at Netherfield, she had to work.

"Good grief, Lizzy! Have you never heard of trading off with someone? Sometimes you are the simplest person!"

* * *

After an early dinner, Jane and Lizzy walked to Netherfield. With double summer time, the road was as bright as it would have been in early afternoon, and Netherfield's red brick façade was soon in view.

When Lizzy saw William, she nearly cried. The dark circles under his eyes and gaunt look were evidence of his exhaustion, but he waved off her concerns and suggested they go for a long walk.

"I actually have some good news," he said as soon as they were clear of the manor house. "Because of my reassignment, I have been given three-days' leave. So I was wondering if you would like to go up to London? Possibly take in a show. I would stay at an officer's club, and you could stay with my mother. What I am saying is that there will be no funny business. What do you think?"

"I am pretty sure I will be able to get the time off." Her supervisor had accused her of being "all work and no play," and it was now her time to play.

"Perfect. But let's not waste the day. Shall we find a place where we can spend the rest of the evening getting to know each other better?" Darcy arched his eyebrows indicating his intentions were less than honorable.

"I might agree to your suggestion if I were one of those Piccadilly commandoes the airmen encounter lurking in London's doorways," Lizzy said, referring to London's most notorious prostitutes, "but I am not. So may I suggest we take a walk through the gardens?"

Darcy didn't budge. "I have spent more time in Netherfield's gardens than the gardener. I know every plant on the estate by name. I know their genus and species." But when he received little sympathy from Lizzy, he yielded. "You drive a hard bargain, but somewhere along the way, may I have a kiss?"

"Just one?"

* * *

Lizzy was looking forward to visiting London as she had not been in town since mid December when, with ration coupons in hand, all the Bennets had boarded the crowded London-bound train at Meryton in the hope of finding something in the shops to give as Christmas gifts, but there was precious little to be had. Except for a scarf for their mother, the clan had returned to Longbourn empty handed, and no one had ventured into London since that time.

"Oh, by the way, I won't be going to Scotland after all," Darcy said as soon as they had taken their seats on the train. "Instead, they are sending me to Yorkshire."

"Oh, balmy Yorkshire," Lizzy said, thinking of the novels of the Brontes and the cold climate and wind-scoured landscape of their books. "You won't have to take your long underwear now."

"I shall warn you, Elizabeth. I have a long memory. If you are to make merry at my expense, I might do the same to you at some future date."

"I am not afraid of you, William Darcy. Under your gruff exterior beats a warm heart."

"That beats for you," Darcy said, taking hold of Elizabeth's gloved hand.

Darcy asked Elizabeth what she would like to do first. He suggested they avoid the area around St. Paul's. It would be a long time before the rubble was cleared, and it made for a rather depressing view, one he wished to spare Elizabeth.

Lizzy asked about an exhibition at the National Gallery. With the gallery's vast collection scattered about the country where it would be safe from Hitler's bombs, the museum had adopted a program of displaying one piece of great art as a morale booster for its citizens. The "picture of the month" program was wildly popular—not for the painting alone—but as a harbinger of better days to come.

"The last one I saw was Rembrandt's *Portrait of Margaretha de Geer*," Darcy answered.

"I saw that as well, but in 1941. Surely, they have changed it by now." Elizabeth gave him a suspicious look. "Not an art lover, are we?"

Darcy explained that as a child, his parents had traveled extensively, leaving him in the care of a governess who would drag him to every museum on the Continent. "Do you have any idea how many museums, galleries, churches, and historical sites there are in Italy alone?" Having never been to the

Continent, Lizzy shook her head. "Thousands. I am at my best on a football pitch."

"All right. No National Gallery. But may we go to Westminster Abbey? I haven't been there since I was a young girl."

"We can go anywhere you like."

After arranging with a porter at Euston Station for their luggage to be sent ahead, they hailed a cab and headed for the Minster, trying to ignore London's bomb-ravaged landscape as they went. Upon entering the Abbey, they were met by one of its guardians—those men who watched over the old Minster, ready to put out any fires if the bombers should return. He and his fellow volunteers had already been through so much. On the night of May 10, 1941, with a bomber's moon guiding the German planes down the Thames, incendiary bombs had fallen on the Abbey. When he had finished telling his tale of the horrors of that night, the gentleman lifted his eyes towards the heavens, stating that he was worried the "flying gas mains" might finish what the bombers had started.

"Flying gas mains?" Lizzy and Darcy asked in unison.

"That is my poor attempt at humor," the man said, chuckling. "Of course, those of us who watch over the Abbey didn't believe it for a moment. Gas mains don't fly nor did we believe the ack-ack gunners had become so good at their jobs that they had successfully shot down one German plane after another."

"Excuse me, sir," Lizzy said, "but we don't know what you are talking about."

"Really? Where are you from? The Outer Hebrides?" Then he apologized for his sharp tone. "Allow me to explain. Two nights ago, more than seventy pilotless planes exploded in the greater London area; the explanation from the government was that they were exploding gas mains. Even to the gullible, it made little sense. After all, we've seen a bomb or two since the Blitz. There's a fair amount of damage throughout the town." After breaking into a devilish grin, he said, "Welcome to London."

"Did you know about these flying gas mains?" Lizzy asked William as they walked towards Poet's Corner.

Darcy, whose squadron had attacked the rocket launch sites, wasn't sure what he could say, but if rockets were falling on London, it was no longer possible to keep Germany's vengeance weapons program a secret.

"They are not gas mains or pilotless planes, but rockets," Darcy explained. "For the last few months, the RAF has been attempting to knock out launch sites in Holland before they could become operational. Because of reports from the Dutch underground, we know where many of them are located. But even with good intelligence, they are damned difficult to find, no less hit. The heavy bombers blanket the area in hopes that they will hit something, but it's really a job for the tactical air force and light bombers." *Or a Mosquito.*

"The guide said that seventy rockets hit London alone." Lizzy was amazed at the number launched in just the one night.

"At this point, I imagine the Germans are just launching the rockets in the general direction of a military target or London in the hope of hitting something important or just to terrorize the civilian population." He was as puzzled as Elizabeth as to the reason why the government hadn't said anything about them. "But let's not talk about rockets while we are standing on Chaucer's grave."

Darcy took Elizabeth's hand. After entwining her fingers in his, he led her to the grave of Samuel Butler, author of *Hudibras*, a satirical poem directed against the Puritans and one of his assignments whilst in school at Winchester.

While Butler, needy wretch, was yet alive,
No generous patron would a dinner give;
See him, when starv'd to death, and turn'd to dust,
Presented with a monumental bust.
The poet's fate is here in emblem shown,
He ask'd for bread, and he received a stone.

Lizzy shared with William that Mr. Butler was

responsible for one of her father's favorite quotes: 'I do not mind lying, but I hate inaccuracy.'"

"Your father has a sharp wit, or so Bingley tells me, and I believe you and your father were cast from the same mold."

"Yes, we were, so consider yourself warned."

Chapter 15

Although the buzzing sound of the rockets was alarming, in the few days since the launch of the first vengeance weapons, Londoners had come to know that it was when the buzzing stopped that death and destruction followed. Lizzy and Darcy had just finished having dinner at the Savoy when they heard the buzzing sound of a rocket above them, and Darcy grabbed Lizzy by the hand and ran with her back into the hotel where its personnel were already directing guests to the basement shelter.

Lizzy found herself seated next to a woman who was dressed to the nines and wearing a diamond broach that could have gone a long way toward rebuilding post-war Britain. The lady, who was old enough to be her grandmother, told Lizzy that if she was going to "pack it in" she would do so in style, and Lizzy smiled at her display of bravado.

"The man at the Abbey told us we were only in danger once the engine stopped," Lizzy whispered to William, "so why did we have to run?"

"Collateral damage. Window glass, debris, and pieces of metal flying through the air can cut a person in half."

"Of course, I knew that," Lizzy answered, feeling perfectly stupid. "I wasn't thinking."

"That's because you are frightened as anyone with the sense of a goat would be." After putting his arm around her shoulders, he realized that Elizabeth was now the most precious thing in his life, and he pulled her closer to him. But after two hours of crouching in the basement of the Savoy singing songs that were popular during the Blitz in 1940 and '41, Darcy suggested they leave the hotel. "The family townhouse isn't that far, and because it has a below-street-level servants' hall, we will be safe there."

Considering that explosions could be heard in the distance, Lizzy felt strange climbing into a cab and wondered if the driver was as frightened as she was.

"Can't you feel the cab shaking?" the cabbie said in answer to Lizzy's question. "This is my third night out in this, but I can't stop driving because of the buzz bombs or my family won't eat. With the Americans gone to France, my trade was already down by half and now this," the driver said, shaking his head. "Most of the bombs are falling south of the river, so I'll just stay north of the Thames. That's where the fares are anyway."

Lizzy was pleased to see William give the man a tip that was larger than the fare, and she kissed him on the cheek to show that she appreciated his generosity.

"Yes, but now I won't be able to pay my mess bill," Darcy complained as he stood in front of the family's Mayfair home, a typical four-story townhouse with an elevated front entrance. Even though decades of coal dust had dulled its white façade and its windows were taped because of German bombs, the residence oozed prestige and money.

"Maybe you could sell one of your slaves to pay your mess bill," Lizzy suggested while looking down into the well of the servants' entrance.

"Unfortunately, we already sold them during the Depression in the '30s," Darcy said as he fitted a key into the lock.

Before the war, when Jane and Lizzy had visited London, they would walk down streets just like this and pretend they lived in one of the townhouses. They would affect posh manners and accents, giggling all the while, and talk about having tea at the Savoy. Yet, here she was, walking into one of these elegant homes on the arm of its future owner after dining at the Savoy.

"Good evening, Mr. Darcy," the butler said as soon as they were in the foyer.

"Hello, Mr. Jackson. Allow me to introduce Miss Elizabeth Bennet of Hertfordshire. She will be staying with us for two nights. I believe my mother saw to the arrangements."

"Yes, sir, everything has been taken care of. Lady Anne is below stairs putting together a tray for the officers in the morning room."

"Where's Macy?"

"Lady Anne telephoned Macy to tell her not to come today. Since the invasion, there are fewer officers to avail themselves of your mother's hospitality, what with all of the gas main explosions."

Jackson raised his eyebrows to let Darcy know he didn't believe that story either.

"Thank you, Mr. Jackson. We shall go down directly."

Dressed in a grey skirt, white blouse, grey cardigan, and wearing sensible shoes, Lady Anne Darcy hardly looked like the daughter of an earl, but even in such plain attire, she was perfectly lovely: tall, slender, with dark hair, blue eyes, and a complexion that would be the envy of someone a decade younger than she. But as soon as mother and son made eye contact, Lizzy knew there was a problem. William's kiss on his mother's cheek was perfunctory. In fact, he seemed happier to see Mrs. Bradshaw, the cook, and gave her a big hug, lifting her off her feet.

"Thank you for ringing, William. I was able to save some dinner for you and your guest," Lady Anne Darcy said while extending her hand to Elizabeth. "Four days after the invasion, I received a letter from the Home Office telling me that our rations would be cut because we would not be entertaining so many military personnel. They were right. I don't think there are more than a dozen up there right now."

"Have you been affected by the rockets?" Darcy asked in a monotone Lizzy found troubling.

"Rockets? I thought they were pilotless planes," Lady Anne said, pointing to the headlines in the newspaper she had been reading. The article included a picture showing a few of the hundreds of barrage balloons whose purpose was to ensnare German bombers. The joke was that without the balloons

England would sink. "But to answer your question, no one on this street was hit, but two nights ago a mews near the park was reduced to rubble and two townhouses in the middle of a row of houses were destroyed—but just those two. Fortunately, everyone had gone down to the kitchen when the first rocket went over, and the ceiling held. It is identical to our townhouse, and knowing that, I do feel a bit better when I am down here."

"Everyone should remain below stairs until this thing is over," Darcy said.

All the while mother and son were speaking, Lizzy had been watching William. Despite his mother living in the midst of this latest attack on London, her son's demeanor was so devoid of emotion that it reminded her of the man she had first seen at The Hide and Hare staring at her with cold eyes, and the thought sent a chill through her.

"I spoke with your father yesterday," Lady Anne said. "As usual, most of the conversation was about the Victory garden. I daresay you would be impressed by the output at Pemberley. Mr. Ferguson has turned your Papa into a first-rate gardener."

There was more small talk about the gardens and the weather, but after tiring of her son's monosyllabic answers, Lady Anne used the excuse of carrying a tray of refreshments to the officers in the morning room to leave the kitchen and told them to help themselves to the leftovers in the refrigerator.

"William, do you think we should return to Hertfordshire?" Lizzy asked after witnessing the uncomfortable exchange.

"Possibly in the morning. But you will be safe down here. I'll bring Georgiana's mattress to the servant's hall, and you can sleep in there," he said, pointing to the room with his chin, "and I can sleep here in the kitchen on a cot."

Before Lizzy could respond, there was a loud explosion nearby, rattling the windows and causing the plates on the table to jump. Before she could say anything, William was up the stairs and out the door. She was about to follow him when Mr. Jackson took hold of her arm and ordered her back to the basement.

"I am an air raid warden, miss, and you must do as I say," he said while putting on his helmet.

"Mr. Jackson, I have Red Cross training. I may be able to help."

"I'll send someone for you if you are needed." The butler followed Darcy out the door.

Lizzy returned to the kitchen to find Lady Anne comforting Mrs. Bradshaw, an elderly lady of about sixty-five years. In contrast to her tense demeanor while talking to her son, William's mother now projected an aura of calm. After offering her cook a glass of water with a sleeping aid in it, she insisted Mrs. Bradshaw go to her room. "I shall be in a bit later," she said in a reassuring voice, and a shaken Mrs. Bradshaw left. Unsure of what to do, Lizzy offered to make tea.

"Yes, that is a good idea," Lady Anne said. "Perhaps just a half a pot as it will only be William and Jackson as I am sure the officers will be needed elsewhere." Her thoughts then turned to her badly shaken cook. "Poor Mrs. Bradshaw. The dear lady thought, as we all did, that with the successful landings in Normandy, this part of our nation's nightmare would be over, but here we are again huddling in our cellars."

Lizzy had no words of comfort to offer Lady Anne. As someone who had not experienced the Blitz, she thought anything she might say would sound trite. The closest she had come was the Luftwaffe's attempt to bomb the Dickinson munitions plant in Hemel Hempstead, but that was more than fifteen miles from Meryton—hardly worth mentioning.

"I was very happy when William called to say he was bringing a friend to town. I guessed correctly that his companion was a female or he would not have called or come here for that matter. You see, we are not on the best of terms at present," Lady Anne said, a sadness obvious in her voice. "I accept full responsibility for our estrangement, except for one thing. William believes that a certain event caused his sister to volunteer for the VADs in Italy. But my daughter, who is very much like her brother, likes an adventure, and because Italy is her favorite place in the whole world, she was keen to go. It had nothing to do with her parents' difficulties."

"William has said nothing to me."

"I am sure he hasn't. I imagine he doesn't talk about me at all," Lady Anne said, biting her lower lip. "Because he is so hard on himself, William thinks everyone can take it. However, most people are not as strong as he is."

"I have seen that side of him as well," Lizzy

acknowledged. "I think because he lost so many friends in the war, he has built this defensive wall around him so he won't get hurt."

"Not get hurt? It is a fool's errand," Lady Anne said surprised that her son could be so unrealistic. "There is no such thing as a defense against heartache. If you love, you will be hurt. The only known cures are kindness, forgiveness, and time, and I know of what I speak."

* * *

Darcy and Jackson did not return for another three hours, and when they did, they were coated in dirt, grime, and plaster dust and smelled of cordite. After the barest of greetings, both headed for the washroom. Knowing the men were safe, Lady Anne told Elizabeth she was calling it a day, but before retiring, she surprised Lizzy by kissing her on the cheek. "You are so lovely, a rose amidst the ruins. William is fortunate to have found you."

As soon as his mother left, William came into the kitchen, and Lizzy wondered if he had been lurking nearby, waiting for his mother to leave. But his only comment was that he was famished and asked if there was anything in the larder.

"I thought you might come back hungry, so I made a few sandwiches for Mr. Jackson and you."

"Mr. Jackson has already gone to bed, so I shall eat them all, that is, unless you want one."

"Your mother and I have been nibbling on Stilton all night, so I'm fine." While preparing his plate, Lizzy listened to William's report of the damage from the rockets. Fortunately, there had been no fatalities, but another pair of townhouses had been damaged. Because they had lost most of their roofs, Darcy declared them to be uninhabitable.

"Whose townhouses were they?" a voice from the shadows asked.

"Come in and join us, Mama."

"I am sorry to interrupt. I was coming out of the lavatory, and I heard you talking about the damage."

Darcy indicated that the rocket had destroyed the roof of the Covington townhouse and had badly damaged a second house to the south of it, but no one had been hurt. Lady Anne gave a sigh of relief, explaining that the Covington family had moved to their country estate in Leicester the previous winter.

"The Home Office requisitioned their townhouse on behalf of the Americans, leasing a whole block of flats for those working in Grosvenor Square. There were so many of them that they had to sleep in shifts," Lady Anne explained. "Of course, the vast majority of them have now gone to France."

After mulling over this information, Darcy indicated that leasing the townhouse to the government was a good idea and suggested his mother contact the Home Office. Lizzy looked at William. If he had any reservations about strangers living in a house that would one day be his, he gave no sign of it.

"People need shelter. Besides, you really need to go to Pemberley—at the very least to get Mrs. Bradshaw out of London. She's aged ten years since I last saw her."

"I don't think your father and I are quite ready for that."

"Ready for what? Staying alive?" Darcy asked, his voice dripping sarcasm. "You told me Papa called yesterday to talk about his vegetables. I imagine the real reason was to tell you to leave London." Lady Anne nodded. "So do as he asks."

"Your father and I are talking, but things are not as they should be."

"Listen, Mama, I know the Germans have stockpiled thousands of these rockets, and there is an excellent chance this will go on for a long time. So as a practical matter, people need a roof over their heads, and you need to go somewhere safe. Sometimes, the best way to help is to get out of the way, so get out of the way."

Chapter 16

Darcy's efforts to maneuver his sister's mattress down the narrow staircase of the townhouse resulted in his burden cascading down a flight of stairs. Waiting at the bottom of the landing was Mr. Jackson. The senior servant had been the Darcy butler for nearly the whole of William's twenty-eight years and had been with the family longer still. Whether in London or Derbyshire, the man always seemed to know when anyone in the family was on the move, and there was no sneaking into the townhouse or Pemberley as long as he was on duty. As a result, Jackson was privy to many of William's secrets from his pre-war nights out on the town.

"For Miss Bennet, I assume?" Jackson asked.

"Yes, it is for Miss Bennet, but I can see to it. Please go to bed, Mr. Jackson."

"I shall return to my bed as soon as the mattress is in place, sir."

Because Darcy wasn't taking any chances with Elizabeth's safety, the mattress was placed under the heavy oak table in the servants' hall. The always efficient Jackson soon returned with sheets and blankets for both of them.

"We should have put the sheets on first," Lizzy said, as the two crawled under the table.

"What fun is there in that?"

"Can you visit awhile or are you too tired.

"If you want, I shall sit up all night with you," he said, squeezing her hand.

"I want to talk to you about your mother."

"On second thought, I *am* tired. We did a lot of heavy lifting helping the wardens search for survivors in the rubble," Darcy said, his words accompanied by the sound of a distant explosion. "I am sure that one was south of the river," Darcy said in an attempt to reassure Elizabeth, but his statement was punctuated by another explosion—this one closer still. "The Germans must be launching the rockets from different locations. I am sure this will go on all night, so please," he said, pointing to the table, "get under the table."

"I'm sure this will sound suggestive," Lizzy said, hesitating, "but will you join me?"

Darcy raised his eyebrows in his best Groucho Marx imitation and smiled, and Lizzy shook her head and wagged her finger at him. After retrieving his cot from the kitchen, he placed the collapsed camp bed next to hers, only the legs of the table separating them.

Once they were both settled, Lizzy laughed at the absurdity of their situation. "'Three days in London,' you said. 'Go up to town and see the sights. Have dinner at the Savoy and go dancing at an officers' club.' You really know how to show a girl a good time."

"Scheduling the fireworks was a little tricky, and I might have overdone it," Darcy said, blowing on his fingers and rubbing them against his shirt, "but you have to admit there hasn't been a dull moment since we got off the train at Euston Station."

"I imagine this is a rather common event for you. The bombs, I mean."

Darcy thought about it for a minute. "That's true. It's not all that different from having flak exploding around a bomber, but I usually don't have my girl with me."

"Am I your girl?"

"I certainly hope so. Otherwise, I have been acting like a complete fool, drooling all over you." Lizzy moved closer so that he might drool. "You do know that if you sleep in your dress, you will be a wrinkled mess in the morning. I could help you out of it."

"William! You shouldn't say such things!"

"If I can't talk about such things, may I think about them?"

"Tell me about a typical raid," Lizzy said, changing the subject.

Darcy was happy to do so. His sexually-laced banter had been an attempt to take Elizabeth's mind off the explosions going on all around them—a difficult thing to do with the smell of cordite seeping into the house. Although his first inclination was to assist the air raid wardens and rescue teams, he knew that to go out into the street meant possibly getting injured or killed, and he was too valuable as a pilot to risk falling victim to collapsing masonry. If he got killed, his CO would probably attach a memo to his file: "Damn fool. What was he thinking?"

"When you are flying through all that flak, what thoughts cross your mind?"

"Truthfully, I do very little thinking as my training kicks in. I rely on my gunners to take care of the night fighters and my navigator and wireless operator to get me to the target. If something goes wrong with the plane, it's the flight engineer's responsibility to fix it. So if I do my job and everyone else does theirs, and if Fate is on our side, we should get home safely."

"I know I would be terrified."

"I happen to think being frightened is a good thing when you are in dangerous situations. I'm very leery of men who say they don't get scared."

"Like George Wickham." Lizzy told him about the American who was squiring Lydia around Meryton as well as Charles's doubts about the veracity of his claims of taking over the second seat after the pilot had been wounded.

"Do you know for a fact that this fellow is actually a gunner? He sounds like a bullshitter to me?" He quickly apologized for his use of a vulgar term.

Lizzy broke out laughing. "Do you really think I would be offended by your saying 'bullshit' while I am hiding under a table trying not to get killed by the Nazis?"

"Nothing is going to happen to you," Darcy said, and he joined Lizzy on the mattress, pulling her to his side and running his hand down her arm and tracing the outline of her hip.

"William, if we keep on like this, I can almost guarantee something is going to happen to me."

"Sorry." Darcy squeezed through the table legs and rolled back onto his cot, placing his hands behind his head so he would not be tempted to act on what was going through his mind.

Returning to the subject of Lydia's suitor, Darcy asked if it would be helpful if he found out more about George Wickham. He explained that there was a mechanic at Helmsley who frequented the American bars because a lot of the Yanks smoked only half a cigarette before putting it out. "Pete empties the ashtrays, and when he gets back to the station, he salvages the tobacco for his own use."

Lizzy mulled over William's offer regarding Wickham and decided it might be a good idea to know more about the American corporal. After all, William wasn't the only one who thought Wickham might be a bullshitter. Charles had hinted at it as well.

Because Lizzy found William's concern for her sister to be so sweet, she wiggled her way from under the table, slipped out of her dress, and removed her stockings. When she went back under the table, she was wearing only her slip and gestured for William to join her under her blanket. "Kissing and touching only, William. Can you do that?"

"I am a trained warrior. I can do anything."

"William?"

"I hope I shall always do exactly what is expected of a gentleman."

"See that you do." Lizzy pulled him to her, and in doing so, they were able to shut out the sound of buzzing rockets and falling buildings—at least for a while.

Chapter 17

"Elizabeth," Darcy said, while pulling on her leg. "Elizabeth, please wake up." But Lizzy was sound asleep dreaming of her handsome warrior's kisses and burrowed deeper under the blankets. Darcy finally gave her leg a good yank, and Lizzy sat up, hitting her head on the underside of the table.

"Sorry about that," Darcy said, kissing the top of her head after she had wiggled out of her hidey-hole, "but you wouldn't wake up."

"What time is it?" When she heard it was only 5:15, she didn't understand why William wanted her to get up so early and tried to shake the cobwebs out of her head.

"I rang Helmsley and was ordered back to the station." After helping her to her feet and draping her shoulders with a blanket, he apologized for the abbreviated holiday. "I would ask that you assist my mother and Mrs. Bradshaw in leaving London. But I shall warn you that Mama can be quite stubborn. If she protests, then just make arrangements for Mrs. Bradshaw to leave town."

While tracing the outline of William's jaw with her finger, Lizzy promised to take care of Mrs.

Bradshaw and to do her best to get Lady Anne to leave as well. "I'll speak with Mr. Jackson about when it would be best for us to go to the train station, so please don't worry."

Darcy slipped his arms around Lizzy and whispered, "Thank you for last night."

"I should be ashamed of myself." After looking at his handsome face, she let out a sigh. "But I'm not."

"I did keep my promise." Lizzy shook her head. "Yes, I did," Darcy insisted. "You do understand what is required. We didn't actually…," but they were interrupted when Darcy heard Mr. Jackson's footfalls on the wooden stairs. From his perch, the butler announced that a cab sent by the RAF was waiting for him.

"Thank you, Mr. Jackson. I shall be right there." After kissing her goodbye, Darcy told Elizabeth that it might be several days before she heard from him again.

"I understand. I really do. Just be safe." Lizzy turned him around and pushed him in the direction of the stairs, but when she heard the door close behind him, tears fell.

* * *

Shortly after Darcy's departure, Lady Anne came into the kitchen and found Elizabeth brewing a pot of coffee.

"I hope you don't mind," Lizzy said, "but I noticed you have more coffee than tea," which was an understatement. The tin of coffee was huge. Because it was Maxwell House, an American brand, Lizzy imagined that the Yanks had donated it to the British Red Cross. "Because we always run short on our tea ration at Longbourn, we now drink coffee with breakfast, and so I have developed a taste for it." With tea nearly impossible to get because of the fighting in the Pacific, the British were turning to coffee to kick off their day even if it was cut with chicory.

"I don't mind at all," Lady Anne answered, "and I would love a cup. Would you like a fresh egg for breakfast?"

Lizzy eyes popped. Although there were chicken coops at Longbourn, the eggs remained rationed, and a driver came by weekly to collect the chickens' output. Her protein-deprived body considered an egg breakfast made with real, not powdered, eggs to be the equal of dining at the Savoy Grill, and she nodded enthusiastically.

"I'm a fair hand at cooking breakfast," Lady Anne said while placing a skillet on the hob. "After the first war, when Sir David came home, I did most of the cooking because servants were difficult to find. They had found jobs during the war with better pay, and they did not want to come back into service. I can't say I blame them."

Lady Anne did have a way with eggs, and the ladies were soon wiping up the last of the yolk with a piece of buttered bread, and Lizzy declared it was a meal fit for a queen. As she washed the dishes, Lizzy noted that Mrs. Bradshaw was having a good rest.

"I gave her twice the normal dose for the sleeping pill. Otherwise, she would have been tossing and turning all night. The downside is that she snores terribly. Usually, if I turn her on her side, she will stop, but I could not budge her last night. As a result, I was awake when William rang Helmsley." After taking a sip of coffee, Lady Anne asked the question she had once had to answer during The Great War: "Are you content to play the role of the girl he left behind?"

"Yes, I am," Lizzy said without hesitation. "But before William left, I promised him that I would do my best to convince you and Mrs. Bradshaw to leave London for Derbyshire."

"Mrs. Bradshaw requires no convincing, and, God willing, she will leave today. But I must stay. Please allow me to explain. Some of the people who were bombed out last night are my neighbors, and they will need someplace to stay. I don't know if you have ever slept in a shelter, but it is a perfectly dreadful experience. But I promise that once they are settled, I shall go to visit my sister who is currently living in Scotland."

"William mentioned Pemberley."

"I can't possibly go there. There is so little room…"

"At Pemberley! My impression from William was that it was huge." Lizzy remembered conversations about an east wing, west wing, conservatory, multiple drawing rooms, study, library, and on and on.

"Pemberley *is* huge, but not the dower house." Lady Anne could see Lizzy had no idea what she was talking about. "Did William not tell you we haven't had access to Pemberley since May 1941?"

With that prompt, Lizzy now remembered a conversation in which William had mentioned that the government had requisitioned the manor house, but she knew little else. The truth was their relationship had been one of fits and starts with only enough time to share little snatches of their personal history. "Our purpose in coming to London was actually to get to know each other better."

"Well, it is my experience that sometimes a few days is enough to find out if you belong together. While in other cases, a lifetime is insufficient to understand your partner. But that is neither here nor there. At present, Pemberley is being used by the government, for what purpose we do not know, except that a security detail patrols the estate, and when my husband goes to the garden, he is accompanied by guards with rifles."

"Rifles! It must be top secret to warrant such protection."

"Oh, it is. With its location so near to the rugged terrain of the Peak District, Pemberley is an ideal location for skullduggery. As a boy, my son liked nothing better than to go on horseback into the District to find some hidden cave or look for bone shards or ancient graves."

As a result of the government's takeover of the manor house, the Darcys had moved into the dower house formerly occupied by Lady Anne's late mother, the Dowager Countess of Stepton. But with Mr. Ferguson, the gardener, and his wife also living in the house, as well as a cook and kitchen maid, it was close quarters, and everyone ate *en famille* in the kitchen.

"What I am trying to say is that it would be a hardship for everyone if I were to go to live there as my husband and I no longer share a bedroom."

Lizzy now understood why Lady Anne did not want to go back to Derbyshire. It didn't take a genius to figure out that she had had an affair that had greatly affected her marriage. Moving back into a house with an estranged spouse was definitely a problem. But she had promised William she would do her best to get his mother out of London, and a promise was a promise.

"Shortly before I left Hertfordshire, my father lectured me on how important it was for me to face up to my fears. In that way, I would be waging my own personal war against Hitler, and when my efforts were combined with a million others, it would contribute to England being victorious."

"May I ask what prompted this lecture?"

"Because I knew William flew missions over Germany, I didn't want to risk being hurt if something should happen to him. My father noticed I was rejecting William's overtures and wanted to know why."

Lady Anne placed her hand on Lizzy's. "Did you lose a lover in the war?"

"No, I didn't. But I did see something awful that caused me to climb into my own protective shell." Lizzy described to Lady Anne the day when the two B-17s collided, killing all twenty men. "Because I had actually danced with one of the men, I thought I should write to his family so they would know he had left behind English friends who were grateful for his service. His mother wrote back and asked that I send a picture of his grave. The next time I was near Madingley, I went to the American cemetery with a Brownie camera and found his grave. I'm sure his mother had pictured something like a manicured gravesite with a headstone, but, of course, it was just dirt, with a temporary wooden cross.

"I had brought flowers with me, but they only served to accentuate the barrenness of the grave. I noticed a young woman was doing the same thing on a nearby grave and for the same reason. It was then that I realized the twenty Americans had been buried all in a row. This girl and I gathered up every flower we could find and placed them on the airman's grave. After taking a picture of his grave, we went to the next one and did the same until we had photographed all twenty. I delivered the photographs to Bassingbourn and left them with the chaplain."

"Oh my dear girl, what a gift you gave those families," Lady Anne said with tears in her eyes. "I had a brother who was killed at Passchendaele in 1917 and is buried in Belgium, and I was unable to visit his grave for two years. I can assure you that I would have greatly appreciated such a gesture."

After mentioning the loss of her brother, Lady Anne went quiet and stared off into the distance. It was only after retrieving a pack of cigarettes from a cupboard and lighting one that she was able to share the tragedy that had befallen the Darcy family.

"My husband's oldest brother, George, was to inherit Pemberley, and if something happened to him, then it would go to the next eldest brother, Stephen. The heir and the spare as it were. Both had been prepared to take on the mantle of the owner of a great estate, but George was killed in the first year of the war at Ypres and Stephen in 1918 in Italy. That left my husband David as the master of Pemberley.

"Because David had two older brothers, he was the carefree younger son, indulged by the whole family. The first time I met him he told me he had gone to St. Andrew's University to study golf, and he was serious."

"How did you meet your husband?"

"At a dance in London," Lady Anne answered, and a light came into her eyes. "I was eighteen years old, and David was nearly ten years my senior. Because he had a well-deserved reputation for being a lady's man, as soon as my mother noted my interest, she whisked me off to the country. But it was too late. I was already in love. We married about fifteen months later. Then the war came, and he was sent to France. The year William was born, 1916, David had been seriously wounded on the Somme and was in and out of hospitals for two years. Miraculously, he recovered, at least enough to play golf, and that was all he really cared about—other than the children and me," she added almost as an afterthought.

"Not Pemberley?"

"Pemberley does *not* have a golf course, and here is Mrs. Bradshaw," Lady Anne said, rising to greet her servant. She immediately informed her cook that she would be leaving on an afternoon train for Pemberley. "I have already spoken to Sir David, and he will see that someone is at the station to meet your train."

"And you, milady?"

"I shall follow in a few days."

"To Pemberley?" Mrs. Bradshaw asked, wide-eyed.

"Yes, to Pemberley. I have been avoiding the situation for too long. It is time to face the music, and I shall be brave and do so." She turned to Lizzy and gave her a knowing look.

* * *

Lizzy stayed in London for another frightening day filled with the sounds of exploding rockets, the reverberations echoing through the city's stone canyons. From the Darcy townhouse, she could see a sky filled with plumes of oily smoke, the result of innumerable fires that were consuming huge swaths of one of Europe's greatest cities.

In bold black letters, newspaper headlines told of the previous day's tragedy at Wellington Barracks. On a beautiful Sunday afternoon, the Guards Chapel had been filled with hundreds of people attending worship service when a rocket had destroyed the chapel, entombing 121 people, its Doric columns, portico, and roof now lying in ruins.

But for Lizzy and Lady Anne, there was little time to discuss the tragedy. They needed to get the house ready for the dozen people who would now call the Darcy townhouse their home. When Mr. Jackson returned from taking Mrs. Bradshaw to the train station, he came with Macy, a servant girl whose job was to help Lady Anne and Mrs. Bradshaw provide food and beverages for the officers. Jackson assured

Her Ladyship that more help would be forthcoming.

"Considering their pitiable situations," Jackson said, "I am sure our visitors will be happy to have a roof over their heads and will pitch in and help."

Rather than reassuring Lady Anne, the butler's statement had the opposite effect as she was made to feel that she was deserting the ship and told Lizzy it would be impossible for her to leave while there was such need in London. "Sir David will understand, so it is your job to make sure William understands as well."

Lizzy, too, felt as if she was fleeing London for the safety of Hertfordshire, but she had no choice. There was a lorry waiting for her at the Meryton Depot, and she, too, had a job to do.

As the train made its way through North London, she observed her bomb-weary fellow travelers. With each passing mile, the passengers became more relaxed. By the time the train pulled into Meryton station, most were talking and laughing with people they had not known a few hours earlier. As Longbourn's façade came into view, Lizzy felt the tension leave her body, but it wouldn't last. When she arrived home, she found a house in turmoil.

Chapter 18

As Lizzy trudged down the drive, suitcase in hand, she envisioned a long nap, followed by a quiet dinner, and then back to bed. Between falling rockets and saying goodbye to William, she was physically and emotionally exhausted and that was before she had arrived at Euston Station for her trip to Hertfordshire. The train station was a sea of humanity, and chaos ruled. Fortunately, Mr. Jackson had anticipated the mass exodus of frightened Londoners and had purchased her ticket when he had delivered Mrs. Bradshaw to the station. With each carriage filled to overflowing, mostly with tearful women and crying children, Lizzy had given up her seat to a mother with her little one clinging to her skirt. By the time she stepped onto the station platform at Meryton, she was sweaty, cranky, and in need of a bath.

As Lizzy entered the Longbourn kitchen, the first person she saw was Jane, who looked completely done in, and Lizzy thought she must be ill or she would have been at work. The second person was her mother, who looked even worse.

"Oh, you have come back, have you, Lizzy? Did you and Flight Lieutenant Darcy enjoy town? There was no question about you going off to London without a chaperone, now was there?" Mrs. Bennet asked, oozing sarcasm. "I hope you had a good time because we are in an upheaval here. My nerves are shattered, and no one seems to care—certainly not your father, who accuses me of all sorts of things, among them, not asking questions. But did he ask *you* any questions before you left, traveling alone with a man your parents have yet to meet? I think not." Without any explanation for her comments, Mrs. Bennet brushed past Lizzy, leaving her to ask Jane what on earth was going on.

"You had better sit down." After taking a deep breath, Jane gave her sister the bad news. "Lydia is pregnant."

"Dear God!" Lizzy said, collapsing into a wooden chair. "I assume it is Corporal Wickham?"

Jane nodded. "As soon as you boarded the train to London, darkness descended in Hertfordshire."

"I am so sorry," Lizzy said, taking her sister's hand. "Please tell me everything."

"Two days ago, the chaplain from Nuthampstead rang to ask if he might call that afternoon to discuss Lydia," Jane began. "Believing that Wickham had asked for permission to marry Lydia, our mother's expectations were high. But the chaplain had a very different reason for coming to Longbourn. Apparently, for the past three months, every time our sister said she was going to study with Maria Lucas, she was actually sneaking out to see George Wickham.

"Lizzy, I am sure you will not be surprised to learn that everything Corporal Wickham told us was a lie. It seems he co-opted another American's life story, using it to get what he wanted from Lydia. When word got back to the man, a Sergeant Lee Masters, he said that if Wickham didn't tell Lydia the truth that he would. But with all the hubbub about the invasion, the sergeant forgot all about it. However, a few days ago, Sergeant Masters saw Wickham in a pub, and it ended in a fisticuffs. Both were arrested by the military police."

"Was Sergeant Masters upset about Wickham *or* Lydia?" Lizzy asked confused.

"Both. The reason the sergeant threw the first punch was because Wickham was bragging that he had," and Jane swallowed hard, "knocked the girl up."

"Oh, no!"

"You can imagine Mum's reaction. After collapsing on the sofa, she called for her smelling salts. You know, the whole routine: blanket, hot water bottle, feet up on the ottoman, etc.," Jane said, the exhaustion evident in her voice. "However, through all this, Lydia was as cool as a cucumber. It seems she has known for more than a month that she is pregnant. She swears when she told Wickham she was expecting, he promised to marry her, so she was in the sitting room with a look on her face as if she was holding the winning cards. But then the chaplain asked her if she was prepared to move, not only across the Atlantic, but all the way to northern California."

"Northern California?" Lizzy asked. "I thought Hollywood was in Southern California?"

"It is, but Wickham had lied about that too. Reverend Barrett gave Lydia additional reasons not to marry Wickham, I mean, other than his being a liar, seducer, and, apparently, a gambler. Our sister shrugged them all off. Then Lydia said the stupidest thing she has ever uttered: She declared that because George is so handsome he could get parts in Hollywood movies like he did before the war and that he would eventually become a film star. The chaplain actually laughed and said, 'How is he going to do that if he lives more than 300 miles away from Hollywood?' And *that* is when Lydia got upset."

Jane described the incredible scene that unfolded. Lydia did not care a whit that Wickham had lied to her about being a waist gunner when he was actually a bomb loader and never left the ground or that all his stories of heroics performed on a B-17 had been gleaned from actual missions flown by others. She didn't care that he didn't know how to ride a horse or that he worked in a sawmill. All she cared about was that he had lied about being in films, and the result was hysteria and copious weeping.

"After finally calming down, Lydia said that because she had been tricked into having sex, she would *not* marry George Wickham. You can imagine Mum's reaction to that statement. And that's when Papa came home." Jane shook her head at the memory. The look on her father's face was one Jane would never forget. "After thanking the chaplain for coming to the house to deliver the bad news in person, he told Reverend Barrett he would see to his family, and the man could not leave fast enough."

Jane explained that Kitty, who had arrived in the midst of the storm, bore the brunt of her mother's anger with Mrs. Bennet accusing the older sister of failing to protect Lydia from such a cad, but Mr. Bennet came to Kitty's defense, stating that all blame rested squarely on Lydia's shoulders. "We gave her good principles to follow," Papa said. "She chose to ignore them."

"Mum kept insisting that Papa make Lydia marry Wickham. When he said he would do no such thing, she started shouting, or maybe it was Kitty who was shouting. It doesn't matter. It was so awful, Lizzy. I never saw the house in such an uproar."

"Imagine what would have happened if I had been

gone for *four* days!" Lizzy said, and Jane let out an exhausted laugh.

"Charles was supposed to come to Longbourn yesterday. Thank goodness he didn't. But I thought it odd that he didn't leave a message. So when the house was finally quiet, I called Netherfield Park, and Mr. Buttons informed me that Charles would not be available for the foreseeable future. I don't understand it at all. It's as if the invasion never happened."

"It's because of the rockets." Lizzy said. After explaining about the rockets raining death and destruction on London and the South of England, she was met with an uncomprehending look. "You know nothing about it?" Jane shook her head. "The Guards Chapel is totally destroyed. The destruction of buildings throughout London is enormous."

Lizzy was an eyewitness to the devastation. On her way to Euston Station, the cab driver had detoured around a block of bombed out flats near Marylebone Road, providing Lizzy with a vision from Dante's *Inferno*: The facades of a row of houses had collapsed, revealing a cross-section of their interiors, still largely intact, except for a bathtub swinging to and fro from a suspended pipe. While firemen hosed down the smoldering ruins, a portable Red Cross canteen distributed hot drinks to the dazed inhabitants of the ruined buildings.

"At lunch, Papa did mention something on the wireless about German planes being shot down. He said that planes had crashed in residential areas, and there was some loss of life. But because of Lydia, I doubt he has read the newspapers in two days."

"Some loss of life!" Lizzy said, her mouth falling open. "With the number of bombs being dropped, there must be thousands of people killed. You should have seen all the people from London getting off the train at Meryton station. I have no idea where they are going, but they are fleeing town in droves, and rightly so."

"Oh, I hope we won't have to take in another family from the East End," Jane said, her face a grimace. "I don't want to appear unfeeling, but wasn't it awful while the Baskers were here?"

"It certainly was challenging," Lizzy agreed. The Baskers, a family of five who had lost everything in the Blitz, had been placed with the Bennets, their individual life experiences creating a chasm between the two families. While the Bennets found it hard to believe that in 1941 there were people living in London who had to be taught how to use a flush toilet and to brush their teeth, the East Enders complained that the Bennets whined about every little thing. When the Baskers departed after six very long weeks, there was a sigh of relief from both families.

"How did you and William get on?" Jane asked.

She was keen to discuss something that did not involve conflict—domestic or international.

"Very well. But because of the rockets, William was ordered back to the station."

"Poor Lizzy. That didn't allow very much time for you to get to know each other."

"Well, it was enough time to find out he is an excellent kisser." Jane and she had a good laugh about that, but then realized they must keep quiet. If their mother thought there was any joy at Longbourn whilst she was so miserable, she would descend on her daughters like an avenging angel.

"Are you in love?" Jane asked.

"I think so, but is it really possible to fall in love so quickly? I know nothing of these things."

"I did," Jane answered without hesitation. She was convinced she had fallen in love with Charles even before they had left the canteen. "We had been together for only two hours, but I knew that this was the man for me."

"My only reservation is his relationship with his parents. Because of the bombs, we spent two hours in the cellar of the Savoy, and, yet, William hardly had a word to say about them. If I didn't know better, I would have thought they were both dead and that his sister was his only living relation, and when he was with his mother, he was so cold to her. It sent a chill through me."

"I don't think it is uncommon for husbands and wives of the upper class to live separate lives or to have little interaction with their children, leaving them to the care of their nurses and governesses," Jane said in an attempt to explain William's behavior.

"Another thing that is not unusual for members of the upper class is to take lovers." Lizzy shared with Jane her belief that both parents had had affairs, but for some reason, William was being especially hard on his mother.

That was to be the last word about Lizzy's adventure in London as a car pulled into the driveway. Mr. Bennet had returned from the uniform factory where he had gone to retrieve Kitty and Lydia.

"Papa will be so happy to see you, Lizzy." But then they heard the chirping voices of the two youngest Bennets. "No rest for the weary," Jane said with a sigh, and Lizzy nodded in agreement.

Chapter 19

Because Lydia considered her older sister to be a scold and an enemy of fun, she was *not* pleased to see Elizabeth and barely uttered a greeting before hastily leaving the kitchen. Kitty, fearing she might also be subjected to a lecture, was hard on Lydia's heels. But Lizzy's concern was for her father who was just now coming through the door.

"Ah, Lizzy, you have returned, a sight for sore eyes," Mr. Bennet said, sitting down at the kitchen table. He looked as if he had aged ten years.

"Jane, dear, make your father a sandwich, will you, please? I have to return to the office. Little work was done today and not because of your absence. I received three telephone calls from your mother, who was on the verge of hysteria, and another from the chaplain, as calm a fellow as I've ever met. But then he has had a lot of experience in informing mothers and fathers of young girls that they are about to become grandparents. In our case, the good reverend was concerned that emotions were running high at Longbourn, and he offered his counsel. I assured him that no blood had been spilt—yet," he said, thinking of his wife.

On his way home, Mr. Bennet had stopped at the uniform family to collect Kitty and Lydia. After hearing of Lydia's pregnancy, Mr. Goode shared the depressing information that he was losing four or five girls every month because of pregnancies. Once he learned a girl was expecting, there were certain jobs she could not do, for example working with dyes. He was convinced some of the girls were deliberately getting pregnant so they wouldn't have to work on the line.

Looking at her father's haggard face, Jane insisted that it was not his fault that Lydia had become pregnant. "If it wasn't Wickham, it would have been someone else."

"No, Jane, you are wrong. It is my own doing, and I ought to feel it. Despite knowing Lydia could not be trusted, I gave her leave to roam High Street. And why did I do it? Because her absence meant I was granted a reprieve from her incessant chattering. And what shall my penance be for neglecting my duties as a father? I shall have to spend the next twenty years raising that wicked man's child."

But there was also good news to share. Mr. Bennet had learned that Sergeant Masters, Lydia's defender, would not be brought up on charges for punching Lydia's seducer, but neither would Wickham be charged.

"I was very glad to hear about Sergeant Masters as I owe the man a debt of gratitude. By landing a punch squarely in Wickham's face, he has saved me the trouble of calling Wickham out. Considering Wickham's heroics took place entirely in his mind, while mine took place on the scarred landscapes of

France, I daresay I would have bested him despite the differences in our ages."

"Papa, a girl having a child out of wedlock is hardly headline news any longer," Lizzy said in an attempt to comfort her father. Not every girl who got herself pregnant was considered to be a tart because, if that were the case, then Meryton was overflowing with them.

Even though she hoped her words would prove reassuring, Lizzy understood why her father was judging himself so harshly. He *should* have taken more care with his youngest daughter, and although she knew his self-criticism was merited, she still felt great sympathy for him.

"Where is your mother? Does she keep to her room?" Mr. Bennet asked. "I imagine she does. The last time she rang the office I shouted so loudly into the telephone that my clerk thought I was having a heart attack."

"What did Mum want?" Lizzy asked.

"She continued to insist that I make Lydia marry Wickham and would not listen to reason. Finally, I had to inform her that our daughter was not the only girl in Meryton who had succumbed to Wickham's charms. She is the only one with child—at least the only one the chaplain knows of. The rascal is now confined to base until his orders come through for a transfer to France where he will no doubt help repopulate that decimated country. But enough about Lydia and the evil Wickham," he said, turning his attention to Elizabeth. "Lizzy, I am glad you are home and away from the rockets falling on London."

"How did you know they were rockets?" Lizzy asked. "There's been no announcement by the government."

"That was true until today. The Air Ministry released details of the 'doodlebugs,' the name assigned by the gunners who are trying to shoot them down. They have a range of 150 miles, weigh 2000 pounds, and can travel up to speeds of 350 miles per hour. I learned this information from a fellow barrister who called me from London with a question about tort law. Tort law! Here we are again under siege, and the man rings me with a question about liabilities with regard to a motor accident. The chasm between the important and the trivial grows wider every day."

But Mr. Bennet was too exhausted to think about ordnance falling on London and reached for his sandwich. After taking a bite, he asked, "And what of your young man, Lizzy? Have you fallen in love?"

"Yes, I have, Papa."

"Will he make you happy?"

"I certainly hope so, but he has not asked me to marry him."

"Nor should he until this war is over and that goes for you, Jane, as well."

After finishing his sandwich, Mr. Bennet excused himself. Before returning to his office, he wanted to visit with their mother. "I am in the mood to annoy her, and it is so easily done."

* * *

As Lizzy unpacked her suitcase, Lydia leaned against the doorframe of her sister's bedroom and asked if she had heard her news about the baby. After she acknowledged that she had, Lydia wanted to know why she did not congratulate her.

"Congratulate you! For getting pregnant?" Lizzy nearly shouted. "I shall not."

"Oh, don't be such a stick in the mud. All will be well," Lydia said with an air of confidence completely at odds with her situation.

"To raise a child without a father is a difficult thing to do, and you will have your hands full."

"Oh, I have no intention of raising my child without a father."

Lizzy stopped unpacking. "What have you got up to?"

"That's for me to know and for you to find out." Lydia turned on her heel and left.

After Lydia's departure, Lizzy thought about all that she had learned about Corporal Wickham. As it turned out, William's instincts about the American had been correct. Wickham *was* a bullshitter, among other things. Unfortunately, his offer of help came too late to save Lydia.

Chapter 20

Shortly after Darcy's return to Helmsley, a ferocious storm hit southern England and northern France. Until the weather cleared over the targets, all scheduled missions were cancelled. Despite being grounded, no pilot was allowed to leave the air station. As soon as the storm passed, the RAF would be back in the air targeting launch sites for the vengeance rockets or providing tactical support for the Allied armies whose progress had been checked in the bocage countryside of Normandy. The ancient hedgerows, impenetrable to both man and machine, proved to be natural barriers to the advancing Allied armies. The war would go on.

Pent up at Netherfield Park, the airmen were eager to telephone their loved ones. As a result, there was an interminable wait as the telephone operator made the connection and the party was summoned to the phone. It was days before Lizzy heard William's voice.

"Listen, darling, this has to be quick because unmarried men are allotted only five minutes," Darcy explained. "Although our time together in London was crazy and far too short, I loved every minute I spent with you. Even with rockets falling, it was the best day of my life. I hope you feel the same way." With her emotions getting the best of her, Lizzy said nothing. "Elizabeth, are you there?"

"Yes, I'm here. I didn't want to interrupt such praise." She listened for William's chuckle, one of the most endearing things about him, and was properly rewarded. "After our night under the table in the servants' hall, I would think you would know how strongly I feel about you." And now it was her turn to chuckle.

Before ending the call, Lizzy told William that his mother had decided to remain in London, and she explained the circumstances. "At first, she thought it would be her neighbors who would be moving into the townhouse, but it turned out to be a family from Lambeth and another from Clapham."

"I shall give credit where credit is due. Unlike some of her neighbors, my mother is not a snob. She wouldn't care where these families were from, that is, as long as they bathe." Lizzy had shared with William stories of the Baskers who didn't want to "waste" water on anything with such temporary benefits as a bath. "But thank you for trying to get her to go back to Pemberley."

"One more thing before you go. If you find the queue for the telephone to be too long, you could use a pen."

"You as well," Darcy quickly shot back, and Lizzy promised to write. The phone was grudgingly passed to Charles, but not before Darcy had whispered that he loved her.

* * *

In the weeks following the invasion, Lizzy had come to dread good weather. Clear skies meant William and Charles would fly missions over France or Germany. Although star-filled nights made it easier for the bombers to locate their targets, it also exposed the Lancasters to flak batteries and aided the night fighters who were up on their perches waiting for them.

While standing on the front steps of Longbourn, watching as one bomber after another flew overhead, Lizzy was joined by her father, but they remained silent as they watched the Lancasters embarking on the first leg of their journey.

"Did you hear about Tommy Wosley?" Lizzy asked about a boy from North Meryton.

Mr. Bennet nodded. "Considering the number of men in service from Hertfordshire, we have been very fortunate in having lost so few from our neighborhood."

"That is true, but, today, I learned that Luke Clyburn is in hospital. He lost a leg in the battle for Caen. Because he will have the use of his knee, Mrs. Clyburn is happy. We receive our good news served up in teaspoons, do we not?"

Their attention soon turned to a Lancaster with a sputtering engine that was turning back toward Helmsley.

"So much of a warrior's life rests in the hands of Fate," Mr. Bennet said, remembering his own time during The Great War and the relief the troops felt when a patrol was cancelled or bad weather prevented the start of a battle. "That particular crew will live to see another day."

"Where do you think they are going?" Lizzy asked, scanning the skies.

"It's hard to say. With the American breakout at St. Lo and the British capturing Caen, they may turn their sights on Germany once again, and their targets will be the factories and military installations that make it possible for the Nazis to continue to fight this war. Even though it is an absolute necessity that our country put the lives of these young men at risk, it doesn't make it any easier when you have a young man in one of those planes."

"I know," Lizzy said, fighting back tears. "But let us talk about something else. For example, where is my family? I came home to an empty house."

Mr. Bennet explained that all of the Bennets had gone to the church for the purpose of putting together boxes containing clothes, tins of food, and other necessities for the people in London and the South of England whose homes had been destroyed by the vengeance rockets.

"Lydia went as well?"

"Yes. Your mother told her that the world did not stop spinning because she got herself in a family way. She did not mince words when she told Lydia that she would have to develop a talent for having several balls in the air all at the one time. She has taken a very different tone with your sister since learning no father will be in the picture. If only your mother—and I—had done things differently, this unhappy business might have been prevented."

Lizzy had given some thought to that as well, but had come to the conclusion that some wartime drama involving Lydia was inevitable as she repeatedly ignored the advice of her older sisters. In fact, she boasted that she was able to screen out anything boring or unpleasant, most especially sermons and lectures delivered by clergy and/or parents.

"I was amazed by what the church ladies were able to gather," Mr. Bennet continued. "Our neighbors must be scouring their attics for every odd and end they can find. I know a balaclava your mother knitted for me when I was in the trenches will find a home in London. I hope all these exertions do not turn out to be busy work like those collections of pots and pans supposedly used for bombers at the beginning of the war. I don't think so much as one saucepan was used for such a purpose."

Lizzy knew exactly what her father was talking about as she had seen huge mounds of pots, pans, tubs, and other metal miscellany poking out from under tarps in a field near Cambridge. Because the government had been keen to involve its citizens in the war effort from the onset, they had hit upon the idea of rubber and metal drives as being the quickest way of doing just that. It was now possible that four years after they were first collected, the contents of that stockpile might end up in a kitchen in Croydon or Kent where some people had lost everything they owned. She also knew how those boxes would be getting to London and shared tomorrow's route with her father.

"What? *You* drive into London! Why not send them by train?"

"Top secret here, Papa," Lizzy said, looking over her shoulder as if someone might actually be prowling the grounds of Longbourn for nefarious reasons. "Two nights ago, a rocket hit a switching station north of London. As a result, everything has slowed to a crawl. The government is concerned about food shortages for those who were bombed out and are eager to avoid a panic. According to William, the Germans have stockpiled thousands of these rockets, so this will go on for a long time. But at least the government has acknowledged their existence."

"Yes, I read a summary of Churchill's speech to the Commons in *The Times*. He said that over 5,000 vengeance rockets have been launched and 17,000 houses have been completely destroyed. I know these people need help, but what do you know about driving in London?"

"Actually, for the past two days, I have been studying city maps with a woman who was bombed out in '40. She will be my trainer, and our destination is a depot in Camden. So that's not too bad."

"Not too bad if a rocket doesn't land on your head."

"But a wise man once told me that an army does not go to war. A *nation* goes to war. This is my job, and I shall do it to the best of my ability."

As the father of five daughters, Mr. Bennet had considered himself blest that he would never have to suffer the loss of a son. But then Mary had been sent to Malta and had been in the thick of it all during the Luftwaffe's nightly attacks on that scarred island. And now Lizzy.

"My girls serve while I sit by my fireplace in my comfortable chair, all warm and cozy."

"As Milton wrote, 'They also serve who stand and wait.'" And her father put his arm around his daughter's shoulder, but he would not look at her because there were tears in his eyes.

Chapter 21

For two weeks, Lizzy wrote faithfully to William every day, but his contribution consisted of one note with the words, "I love you. Hope everyone is well" written in a less than perfect hand.

"Obviously, this is something he has no interest in doing," Lizzy complained to Jane.

Jane was equally despondent. "I do wish we could go to Netherfield Park to see William and Charles," Jane said, pouting. "I wonder why they stopped allowing friends and family to visit."

"Security, I imagine. Think of all those propaganda posters: 'Be like Dad, keep Mum?' and 'Tell nobody—not even her,' implying that women cannot keep a secret."

Jane started laughing. Although the message was serious, some of the propaganda posters were ridiculous.

"My favorite is, 'Keep mum. She's not so dumb,' with that femme fatale who looks like Betty Grable lying on a couch in her slip with *three* men staring at her."

"Why would any woman want three men in her

life?" Lizzy asked. She was having enough difficulty with just the one.

"I believe, in her case, there were many more than just the three men," Jane answered, and the sisters burst out laughing.

"But when you think about it, you and I are actually quite fortunate. Most sweethearts, mothers, and wives of men in service do not get telephone calls from their loved ones, even infrequent ones. It's only because William and Charles are flyers that we are able to talk to them at all."

But Jane wasn't having it, and while she vented her frustration over a war now in its fifth year, Lizzy's thoughts returned to those poor souls in London and the southern counties where each day brought more rockets, more death, more destruction. In that light, being barred from Netherfield seemed trivial in comparison.

* * *

Although Jane had been fortunate to receive the occasional call from Netherfield Park, Lizzy had heard nothing from William. But when the telephone finally rang, the call came from Skipton in Yorkshire.

"Elizabeth, I'm sorry I haven't rung you," Darcy began, "but the reason is that I am no longer at Netherfield, but in Yorkshire, and I've already started my training. Would it be possible for you to come to Skipton this Saturday as I have the afternoon off and all of Sunday as well?"

"I think I can manage it." She had already spoken to her supervisor about just such a contingency.

"I'll book a hotel room for you."

"But where will *you* stay?" Lizzy asked with some concern as she thought of their night together under the table at the Darcy home in London and the liberties taken with no resistance from her. But everything had changed with Lydia's news about the baby. They had been playing with fire, and if they continued to do so, they would get burned.

"Don't worry. I have a curfew, so you're safe from me—for the time being anyway," he added. "I'll send you all the details by post."

* * *

When Lizzy stepped onto the platform at the railway station in Skipton, the gateway to the Yorkshire Dales, she found William waiting for her. It was a gorgeous late summer day. After the debacle of their time in London, she considered it to be an auspicious start to their two days together.

"You look beautiful," William said, after giving her a quick kiss on the lips.

"Beautiful? In my traveling coat? Surely, you are exaggerating."

"You would look beautiful in a burlap sack."

"I doubt that, William. But I thank you nonetheless. You, on the other hand, look very tired."

"Oh, they run us ragged, but I'll tell you more about that after we get you settled."

With its worn carpets, thinning upholstery, and dusty lamps lighting the registration desk, The Shorn Sheep, a large wood-framed establishment on the village's main thoroughfare, had seen better days. It

170

was likely that at the time of The Great War it had seen better days. Everywhere she looked there was an air of Victorian decrepitude, including Victorian Era dust forming swirled patterns on the wood furniture.

"Is it all right?" Darcy asked. "Will it do? It was the only place that had a room left. I didn't make allowance for the hordes fleeing London. The town is full of refugees."

"It was the same way on the train." Lizzy had thought most people would get off in Leeds where there would be more housing, but they hadn't. "Don't worry. I was a girl guide, and I am used to roughing it."

"According to the proprietor, Mrs. Aldersgate, the entire hotel was refurbished between the wars."

"That could be anytime between 1919 and 1939. Are you saying that it is possible my mattress and I may be the same age?" Darcy indicated that Mrs. Aldersgate had not been specific as to dates. "Oh, who cares about a mattress when I am here with you?" Lizzy said, kissing his cheek. "Let's register so that I can get rid of this suitcase, and we may go out into the great outdoors."

After dinner, the couple walked to the edge of town to watch the sun closing out another day in the Yorkshire Dales. Lizzy, who had never been farther north than the Peak District, and that in bad weather, was in awe of the scenery: a vast rolling landscape that disappeared into the horizon.

"I don't think I have ever seen a more beautiful view," Lizzy said while looking at the undulating hills.

"I have."

"At Pemberley?"

"No, while looking at you." Lizzy thought she would melt.

"Speaking of Pemberley, why did you not tell me about the clandestine activities going on at the manor house?"

"Oh, Mama told you about the ju-ju men, did she?"

"Ju-ju men?"

"That's what everyone in my survival class called them. No one knows for sure, but I believe Pemberley's temporary guests were *agent provocateurs* whose future included being dropped into Nazi-occupied Europe."

"You never told me about your survival course either."

Darcy detailed the survival training required of all airmen in the event it became necessary for a crew to abandon their plane behind enemy lines. After the airmen were dropped off at different locations in the Peak's rugged terrain, they were told to make their way back to the airfield at Ringway near Manchester. They were easy pickings for the ju-ju men with their blackened faces and specialized training, and when captured, the trainees had been treated badly.

"At our debriefing, one of the chaps asked why we hadn't been warned about the ju-ju men, and the instructor said in a voice straight out of a Great War movie: 'You were dropped behind enemy lines, and you didn't think you would be pursued?' So a few days later, back we went. Of course, I saw a ju-ju man behind every tree or rock, and it took me a bloody twelve hours to get back to the rally point."

"But there were no ju-ju men following you, were there?" Lizzy guessed.

"Not a one," and they both started laughing. "But then I went to Scotland and did it all over again."

"Why?"

"I didn't think if I was shot down it would be in an area I would be familiar with. Although British pilots have been shot down over England, it's not the usual scenario."

"Oh, look, the hills are glowing," Lizzy said, wishing to end a topic of planes being shot out of the sky. Darcy stood behind Lizzy, wrapping his arms around her waist. When she looked up at him, he kissed her. Although he had done a fair amount of kissing in his time, there was nothing like Lizzy's lips to remind him of how pleasurable kissing could be, and he couldn't wait for a time when he would be able to make a habit out of it.

"There's a mattress back at the hotel that needs testing," Darcy whispered while kissing her neck.

"How true, and I *am* tired. Thank you for thinking about me and not yourself."

"My pleasure," Darcy said, frowning.

* * *

As Darcy lay on his biscuit, the awful bedding provided to military men everywhere in the Empire, he hoped Elizabeth was having a better night than he was. Because of Elizabeth, his mind would not settle as he was imagining them together in his bedroom at Pemberley making love on a soft feather bed with a full moon serving as their only light. They had also made love in his mother's huge canopied bed and in the gardens at Pemberley, and to duplicate a delightful night in London, under the table in the servants' hall. But all this love-making was leaving him less than satisfied.

Darcy sat up and lit a cigarette. Knowing Elizabeth had never been with a man, he realized that some of the things he had said to her were improper, but he had been thinking and waiting for her for so long—not some idealized woman, but specifically Elizabeth Bennet. When Darcy had looked up from his pint at The Hide and Hare and saw her glorious dark eyes, he had a feeling he had seen her before. When he met her again at Netherfield Park, he knew it. It had been during the summer of 1942, and they had shared a lifeboat.

While floating in a dingy on a roiling ocean, Darcy remembered receiving a progression of visitors like a king in his court. His Grandmother Fitzwilliam was the first to arrive. Because his parents were frequently gone from Pemberley, it was Jeanne Devereaux Fitzwilliam, the Dowager Countess of Stepton, who had overseen the rearing of the children, and her devotion to them was rewarded with their deepest affection. Various friends and relations had followed his grandmother, including his parents and sister, but the final person to join him in his raft was unknown to him: a dark-haired beauty with eyes as black as the moonless Atlantic. It was she who had convinced him not to go into the water. "You don't want to do that, William," she had said in a soothing voice. "A ship will soon be here to take you back to England." Following her instructions, he had remained in the raft because he wanted to live so that he might be with her.

Once in hospital, he understood that this lady, Neptune's daughter, was a hallucination. But that didn't matter. It was an illusion that had saved his life. In the months following his recovery, he had dreamt of his visitor frequently, but over time and because of imminent dangers, the memory had faded until he thought no more about her, that is, until he had met Elizabeth Bennet. In her, an idealized figure became flesh and bone.

Darcy took another Players out of the pack and lit it with the glowing ember of his cigarette. If it hadn't been for the war, he would already have proposed to Elizabeth, but war complicated things. When he arrived in Yorkshire, he was told his group of Pathfinders would be assigned missions for very specific targets: canals, dams, factories, prisons, Gestapo headquarters, troop barracks, and mansions occupied by high-ranking officers. The RAF wanted to make it so personal that the Germans would know they weren't safe anywhere.

In most cases, to avoid German radar, the planes would fly at roof-top level, but in flying so low, they would be easy targets for German artillery. Even so, he felt his odds of returning from a mission as a Pathfinder were no worse than flying a Lancaster over Berlin or through the Ruhr Valley peppered with 88s.

He wasn't worried about himself; that was pointless, as war was a crapshoot. Darcy's concern was for Elizabeth. Because of the danger, she had tried to push him away, but he had so overpowered her with his love that she had succumbed. Even so, she had asked that they not talk about marriage until after the war, and he had agreed. Despite the restrictions, he had no doubt her feelings matched his own as he could feel the power of her love even when they were apart.

It was a given that as soon as victory was declared, Elizabeth and he would marry. All he had to do was survive.

Chapter 22

After a breakfast consisting of watery oatmeal in the hotel dining room, William and Elizabeth arranged for a picnic lunch to take with them into the Dales. With petrol rationed, they would join a half dozen others riding in a charabanc pulled by two giant Belgian horses. Lizzy was thrilled by the adventure, Darcy less so.

"I have flown over the Dales numerous times, and it is a landscape almost devoid of human habitation. And, yet, here we are in the midst of a mob," Darcy said as they waited for the wagon to arrive.

There were times when Darcy's privileged background came to the fore, most especially when he had to wait—for anything.

"Did you really think we would have Skipton all to ourselves?" Lizzy asked, teasing him. "The village is known as the Gateway to the Dales. Thus, it would be reasonable to expect that Skipton would be crowded on the weekend. However, my impression is that you have spent little time in Skipton which would account for the surprised look on your face when you saw the interior of The Shorn Sheep."

"I'm sorry about that hotel. I left it to the mess

sergeant who told me he got the last room in the village. How did you sleep?" he asked, hoping for an answer that didn't include bedbugs.

"I like it when a mattress curls up around me. Very cozy," Lizzy said and then nudged him so he would not feel too bad. "Have you never been to Skipton before?"

"Not since the war started. The truth is, after a full day of training, I'm too tired to go anywhere. I am either in my room or in the mess."

Lizzy asked about William's training on the Mosquito. She knew his training on the Lancaster had taken place over the plains of central Canada, but because he was already a qualified pilot, she wondered what was involved. "Obviously, not everything is new to you. After all, you *are* a pilot."

"That would be a logical assumption, but there's very little that happens in the military that is logical. My instructors don't seem to care about my years of experience or the number of missions I've flown or they haven't bothered to read my file as I am very nearly treated as a raw recruit. It's bloody annoying."

The first two weeks of Darcy's training took place in the classroom. Because the Mosquito was manned by a two-man crew, pilot and a flight engineer, it was necessary for both airmen to have knowledge of the other's position in the event of an injury or a disabled ship. As a result, Darcy had to learn—again—how to read charts and map out a course in the event something happened to his flight engineer and navigator, and the flight engineer had to have rudimentary knowledge of how to fly the plane.

"After completing the navigation course, the stunts began. In order to see how you function when you are sleep deprived, three hours after lights out, some idiot wakes you up by banging pots and pans outside your window or you may be subjected to freezing temperatures before being put behind the controls of the bomber. It's as if I am back at Cambridge in my first year enduring initiation rituals. I keep waiting to be short-sheeted."

"Does any of it help to make you a better pilot?"

"No, it's ridiculous," Darcy answered, spitting out the words. "What men who fly desks don't understand is that it is fear that keeps you alive. When you are afraid, the body releases adrenalin that allows you to do things you never thought possible, like flying a lumbering bomber while trying to shake off a sleek night fighter bent on your destruction. The RAF cannot duplicate that, but it doesn't stop them from trying."

As Darcy talked, Lizzy watched as a second charabanc filled with tourists pulled away, and she knew William's patience was running thin. If they didn't get on the next one, he might very well commandeer the wagon. But then they heard someone calling his name, and a fellow member of the RAF crossed the street and took hold of Darcy's hand.

"Look at you!" Darcy said, while pumping the man's hand. "Miss Elizabeth Bennet, this is my flight engineer, Sergeant Mickey Edwards, formerly of Liverpool!"

"Hat's off to you, sir, for being one of the chosen few," the sergeant answered in a nasal Scouser accent, proof that he was a true Liverpudlian. "What are you two up to today?"

"We are waiting for the next charabanc to take us into the Dales. Would you like to join us?" Lizzy asked.

"I'd love to." Then Edwards started to laugh. "I'm only teasing, sir. Just wanted to see your face when I said I was coming along, and it was worth it. I thank you for the offer, Miss, but soon enough, I'll be sharing a small space with Mr. Darcy, so I'll take a pass. Speak to you back at the station, sir. Have fun!"

With a little elbowing, Darcy made sure that the third charabanc was the charm, and they were on their way. Because Darcy had seen enough of the Dales from his Mosquito, he was more interested in a quiet spot for a picnic. But whenever the charabanc stopped, the couple found the green landscape swarming with picnickers. When the wagon made a turn heading back in the direction of Skipton, Lizzy suggested they walk back to the village.

"It can't be more than three miles, and I am sure that somewhere between here and there we shall find the perfect place to eat our lunch."

"Will the leather on your shoes hold up?"

"Yes, of course. I came prepared to do a lot of walking and packed accordingly." She looked at her brown boots and declared that only walking shoes could be so ugly.

The spot they found was on sloping ground far enough from the main road to provide some privacy and as a buffer against the endless wind. With the exception of an occasional walker with staff in hand, they were finally alone. While Darcy spread a blanket and emptied the picnic basket, Lizzy relished the sounds of nature, sounds that were disappearing from Hertfordshire. Even before the arrival of the RAF and American Air Corps, the short distance from Longbourn to central London, where her father had practiced law for twenty years, made Meryton a near suburb of London. With its transformation, a price had been paid: the luxury of silence.

"I love it here, William," Elizabeth declared after being summoned to join him on the blanket.

"And I love you." Darcy said, putting down his sandwich and pulling Lizzy to him. "Thank you for coming."

"How could I resist with all this beauty before me? I would have been a fool not to come."

"Is that the only reason—the scenery?"

"No. I came because I am so in love with you that, if necessary, I would follow you to the ends of the earth. You are all I think about. While I am driving the lorry, you are in the cab with me. When I am waiting at the depot or on the farms or delivering supplies, I imagine you by my side. The whole time I am on the road, I talk to you as if you were there in person. It's as if you have always been a part of my life."

"You feel that way because we have been together for longer than you know."

Lizzy removed the hand that had been resting on her thigh. "What does that mean? 'Longer than I know?'"

After hesitating, Darcy revealed to Elizabeth how

she had been with him in the life raft after he had ditched his Hurricat. "You were the reason I didn't go into the ocean."

"But when you flew the Hurricat, you didn't know me," Lizzy said confused. "How can you say it was me who was with you?"

"I can't explain it, but when I looked up at you at The Hide and Hare and saw your dark eyes, memories of that night returned, and when we were out in the gardens behind Netherfield, I was absolutely sure that you were my visitor."

"William?" Lizzy said, shaking her head.

"I'm not making this up, Elizabeth. If you hadn't come to me that night, I *would* have gone over the side, and I *would* have drowned. And because of that, I know that you and I are destined to be together— forever."

"I don't know what to say, except that I believe you," she said, slipping her arm into his. "And if it is Fate who has determined that we are to be together, then I think we shall never be apart. Considering that I am leaving tomorrow for Meryton and you will be flying missions, I know that statement sounds stupid."

"No, it doesn't. I know exactly what you mean." Darcy took her in his arms, and in one easy motion, she was lying on her back, and she pulled him on top of her. As Lizzy felt him move against her, she whispered, "Soon."

Chapter 23

"Shall we walk? Get away from the crowds?" Darcy asked after enjoying a steak and kidney pie, with an emphasis on the kidneys, in one of Skipton's most popular public houses. "It's a beautiful night. Let's not waste it by staying indoors."

"Are you luring me into the dark, sir?"

"Yes, I am. Unfortunately, with so many people about, we will be limited to star gazing, that is, unless I can find a secluded spot where I may kiss you without interruption."

Lizzy laughed. "Don't you think there was enough kissing for one day while lying on the blanket?"

"There is no such thing as enough kissing."

After putting a fair distance between the lights of High Street and themselves, a thousand points of light emerged from behind feathery wisps of clouds. There were so many stars that it looked as if handfuls could easily be snatched from the night sky.

When they were free of the noises of the village, Lizzy broached the subject that had been on her mind since meeting Lady Anne Darcy. She didn't like the idea that William was estranged from his mother.

"I received a letter from your mother thanking me for my assistance while I was in London."

"Yes, she wrote to me as well. She said your help was invaluable."

"Your mother had nice things to say about me, and you didn't tell me?"

At first, Darcy didn't answer. He knew Elizabeth was unsettled by the chilly relationship between mother and son and wanted to talk about it. Although he didn't, he decided to get the subject out of the way.

"I like your mother very much."

"That is because Mama is very likable. In fact, when Georgie and I were children, we liked no one better. She was our riding master and quizzed us on our French lessons. She taught us to swim, and we picked apples together. At bedtime, she would tell us stories or read books to us. When I was at Winchester, she visited regularly—one of only a handful of mothers who did." Having nothing else to add to the list, Darcy went quiet.

"But then she had an affair."

"Yes. She had an affair," Darcy said. "Considering my father's dalliances began a few years after Georgie was born, one might say that Mama was only doing what her husband had been doing for years. However, my father's affairs were usually brief and primarily sexual. On the other hand, my mother's affair was no sexual tryst. She fell in love with Captain Brown, an Australian naval liaison officer to the British Navy, and asked my father for a divorce.

"What followed was entirely predictable. Her brother, Lord Fitzwilliam, came down on her like a ton of bricks. A divorce would shame the family, and if he had to endure being married to a woman he refers to as the 'Evil Eleanor' in order to avoid harming the family's reputation, she would have to stay married to Papa. He advised her to go back to her husband before it became a scandal. But it was too late. Word had already got out. The captain was sent back to Australia, my father retreated to the dower house at Pemberley, and my mother to the townhouse. At the risk of making my father a sympathetic character, I shall tell you he was devastated by my mother's attempt to dissolve the marriage. He could hardly believe his wife wanted him out of her life."

"And because of your mother's actions, you felt betrayed."

"Of course I felt betrayed. My mother wasn't just divorcing her philandering husband. She was taking a sledgehammer to her family."

"With you and Georgiana grown, is it possible your mother felt she had raised her family and that it was her turn to be happy?"

"You are making excuses for my mother violating her marriage vows," he said in an accusatory tone.

"No. That is *not* what I am saying. Your mother is no less guilty than your father, but at the time your mother became involved with Captain Brown, there were a lot of things going on in her life. Her husband was having multiple affairs, there was a war on, her children were grown and no longer needed her, and she wasn't getting any younger. She was probably feeling she had given her all to her family, and it was now her time."

Lizzy waited for William to say something, but he remained silent, looking off into the distance.

"What your mother did was wrong, and I know you are deeply hurt. But because she fell in love with a man who was not your father does not mean she stopped loving her children."

"Would you be so understanding if this happened to your parents?"

"I can't answer that because there is no infidelity in my family, but that does not mean there are no problems."

Lizzy described her parents' marriage as a union of opposites. While her father was an intelligent man, a magistrate, who valued reasoned debate, her mother was an impulsive woman who gave little thought to the consequences of her actions. Despite his superior intelligence, rather than guiding and correcting, Mr. Bennet elected to sit back and watch as his family made their own way, and in at least one case, with tragic consequences.

"Lydia is pregnant by Corporal Wickham," Lizzy said, sharing the awful news with Darcy for the first time. "Everything Wickham told her was a lie, including flying on a bomber and his having acted in films."

"Do you want me to go to Nuthampstead and give Wickham a good thrashing?" Darcy asked in all seriousness. "Or I can arrange to have it done. The same mechanic who culls cigarettes from the Yanks is quite capable of pulverizing an opponent."

"Thank you, but 'no.' Other than providing support for the child, Wickham is out of the picture. Because he never acted in a film and will never be a Hollywood star, Lydia will not marry him."

After mulling over that information, Darcy said, "It's easy for me to say this because Lydia is not my relation, but why would you want your sister to be married to a liar?"

Lizzy had come to the same conclusion. "I believe this sad event happened because my parents were lax in their disciple. Although I am disappointed in my father's cavalier approach to parenting and my mother's lack of judgment, I still love them."

"But the reason you are able to forgive your parents is because you are a better person than I am."

"*No, I am not,*" Lizzy protested. "Perhaps, because I am a woman, I understand your mother better than you do. When your mother was in the midst of the affair, she wasn't thinking because she was experiencing all those wonderful feelings of the first blush of love. I know this because it is happening to me. I am more alive than I have ever been in my whole life. Every sensation I feel, I feel doubly because of you. It is both wonderful and terrible and that is what your mother felt for a short time with a man who reminded her of the joys of being in love.

"I want to say one more thing, and then I promise to mind my own business. My parents have been married for twenty-five years, and they are still in love, but their affection for one another is not obvious to those around them. When I marry, I don't want to have to search for clues that my husband loves me. I want it out there for all the world to see."

Darcy took both of Elizabeth's hands in his. "You have asked that I not talk about marriage until after the war, but allow me to say this: When we marry, there will not be one day that goes by that you will not know how much I love you. Because you are as much a part of me as my heart and my soul, you will never have to guess how I feel about you."

Lizzy flung herself at Darcy with such force that he nearly went down, and they both started laughing. Overwhelmed by his words, she began to cry, and through her tears, she told him, "You have my permission to say such things every day of my life."

Darcy picked her up and swung her around and then kissed her. "Because you have asked, I shall write to my mother, and when I am in London, I shall call at the house and be civil. Will that satisfy?"

"And your father?"

"Good grief! Are we to have the father talk as well?"

"I can't help but wonder what he is like."

"My father could charm the socks off of you. I, on the other hand, in a similar situation, would begin with other articles of clothing, starting with this." He began to unbutton her coat, but as he did, a couple came out of the dark. As the pair passed, the man doffed his hat and chortled, "Good luck, laddie."

"They must be newlyweds," the lady on his arm said.

"If they were newlyweds, why would they be standing out here in the chill? They'd be in their room, warming the bed." The woman started laughing, and Darcy and Lizzy did the same.

"The man does have a point. Why are we standing out here in the cold when you have a nice warm room at The Shorn Sheep?"

Lizzy shook her head. "Because Lydia is on everyone's mind, before leaving Longbourn, I promised my mother I would behave myself. So we must wait."

"There are times when I think this war will never end," a frustrated Darcy answered.

"Eventually, the war *will* end," Lizzy said, turning him in the direction of Skipton. "But until it does, I shall follow my mother's advice and keep my knees together."

Chapter 24

Lizzy walked into a dark and empty kitchen. With the sound of laughter coming from the sitting room, she knew her mother was listening to *It's That Man Again*, her favorite radio program, and Lizzy's as well. But she was more in need of food than fun, and she lifted the lid of the pot simmering on the stove and found what had become a wartime staple: red cabbage and potatoes with a ham bone added for flavor. But she was hungry and the soup warm, and by the light of a 40-watt kitchen bulb, she ladled the pot's contents into a bowl.

"No need to eat in the dark. The blackout shades are drawn," Mr. Bennet said while entering the kitchen and turning the switch. "If you don't mind, Lizzy, I'll have a bowl as well."

Although she understood her father didn't want her to eat alone, she wasn't sure she wanted the company. Since returning from Yorkshire four weeks earlier, she had driven her lorry into London filled with fresh food, tinned food, dried food, blankets, clothes, and pots and pans that had been extracted from an enormous stockpile near Cambridge as if it were a kitchenware quarry.

Despite the exhausting schedule, Lizzy was glad to be kept busy. After completing his training near Skipton, William had been sent to a station in Wiltshire. Although he was prevented from saying anything, she understood he was flying a lot of missions. Except for the rare telephone call and a few field-service postcards, she had only the warm memories of their time together in the Dales to tide her over until she saw him again. Although she would have cherished a love letter, when he rang her, she didn't complain as he always sounded exhausted.

"You look completely done in, my dear," Mr. Bennet said.

Lizzy nodded her head. Although she drove to the same warehouse in Camden every day, she never went by the same route. Because of the debris from the rockets and the crews repairing the streets or people running out in front of her lorry, Lizzy had to be on high alert every minute she was behind the wheel.

"It's exhausting work. But I don't want to talk about it. It sounds as if I'm complaining when I shouldn't be."

She also didn't want to talk about the war. The newspapers were filled with reports of British, American, and Polish casualties incurred in an attempt to end the war quickly by going into Germany by way of Holland. After weeks of fierce fighting, it appeared that General Montgomery's daring plan had failed as the last bridge to be crossed at Arnhem remained in German hands.

"Well, if you want to take your mind off your

own troubles, you might comfort Jane as Charles's squadron has been transferred to Yorkshire, and Helmsley is to be shuttered. But I'm surprised they are sending the Lancasters north, farther away from the action in France and Holland."

Lizzy wasn't surprised, and she shared news from London: The Germans had launched a second, more advanced, vengeance weapon that went faster and farther than the buzz bombs and made no noise. Several of the workers at the depot have seen these silent terrors whoosh by.

"The fact that you can't hear them coming has greatly enhanced the fear factor which, of course, is exactly what Hitler wants."

"So the RAF is moving their bombers to bases where they will be out of range of these rockets," Mr. Bennet surmised. "That makes sense."

"Please let's change the subject," Lizzy said, staring into her bowl. That day she had seen a gruesome propaganda pamphlet dropped over London by the Germans that showed the results of a British air raid on Hamburg, and she was trying to get the images of rows of burnt bodies lying in contorted positions out of her head. "Do you have any good news to share?"

"Actually I do. Lydia and Kitty are not at home, so the house is quiet." Mr. Bennet explained that because so many of the local girls were with child, the Americans were holding classes to educate the expectant mothers on what they could expect from the American government. "Despite Lydia's protests that I remain at home, I walked with her to the school because when Lydia protests, you know something is not right."

"And what did you learn?" Lizzy asked. What trouble could an obviously pregnant eighteen-year-old girl possibly get into?

"Behind the scenes, your sister has been busy. She arranged to meet her knight in shining armor, Sergeant Masters, to help her with the paperwork for the allotment. Wickham is to have a certain amount deducted from each pay voucher, and if he should be killed, the baby will be his beneficiary."

Lizzy digested this information with her soup. "I really want to kick Wickham where it hurts, but I wouldn't wish him dead."

Mr. Bennet withheld his opinion.

"In talking to Sergeant Masters, I thanked him for defending Lydia's honor," Mr. Bennet continued. "As a measure of my thanks, I warned him of a plot in the making. When I told him that Lydia was determined to have him as her husband, he said he had been around the block a few times and that I need not worry. He was there merely as Lydia's friend."

Lizzy informed her father of Lydia's statement that she had no intention of raising the baby by herself. "She is out to trap Sergeant Masters."

"My impression of Sergeant Masters is that he will either avoid the trap entirely or deliberately jump into it. As he said to me, he is no 'pushover,' and he's twenty-five years old—old enough to know when a girl is trying to ensnare him. But we have news from your sister Mary as well. Apparently, you are to be an aunt twice over."

"Oh my God! Mary's pregnant?" Lizzy thought she would be ill. Once news got out that Mary was expecting, everyone in Meryton would think the Bennet sisters were a family of harlots.

"But this is good news. It seems your sister married Corporal Robert Kett of Norwich nine months ago. Because she thought her family would criticize her for marrying someone on such short acquaintance, she kept her clandestine marriage under her bonnet. For the past six months, Corporal Kett has been in the fight on the Italian mainland, but when he was wounded, Mary was allowed to visit him in the hospital in Rome. We expect the result of that reunion to arrive sometime in April. I imagine the hospital beds have screens around them or your sister isn't as shy as I thought," Mr. Bennet said, chuckling.

"Papa, I can't believe you said that! You don't think they... Surely not in the hospital!" But thinking of William, she started to laugh. That is something he would do—or at least try to do. "Will Mary be coming home to have the baby?"

"Actually, no. She is currently living in a convent in Rome. The sisters take care of two hundred orphans, and Mary is assisting them. When you are rested, you should read her letter. It is filled with hope and joy and good tidings. It will lift your spirits."

"Well, I look forward to reading it, and on that positive note, I shall go comfort another sister whose spirits need lifting."

"Any news from William?" Mr. Bennet asked over his shoulder.

Lizzy shook her head. "But I imagine he's flying

missions against the Germans in Holland. Of course, he can't say. I'll just be glad when all of this is over."

* * *

After consoling Jane, who was already making plans to travel to Yorkshire to see Charles, and advising her where *not* to stay in Skipton, Lizzy headed for her bedroom. She wanted to be dreaming of William before Lydia came home. Because she had lingered too long with Jane, Lydia found her.

"Hello, Lizzy. Did Papa tell you where I have been?" Lizzy nodded, giving her sister no encouragement. But a lack of interest never stopped the youngest Bennet sister from sharing. "While I was at the church, I met Sergeant Masters. He was the one who defended my reputation when Wickham told such lies about me."

"Lydia, you can stop pretending your meeting with the sergeant was accidental. Sergeant Masters told Papa you had asked him to go. Apparently, he has a fondness for the truth."

"Why shouldn't I ask him? He likes me very much," Lydia hissed. "And I would appreciate it if you would take that sour look off your face. You are just jealous because you came back from Yorkshire without an engagement ring."

"The reason I am not engaged is because I actually try to plan for the future," Lizzy answered. "I have told William I have no wish to discuss matrimony until the war is over."

"Oh, is that the reason you haven't seen him since Yorkshire?" Lydia asked, smiling sweetly. "But I don't want to quarrel with you. Sergeant Masters is to come to tea on Sunday, and he is bringing two friends."

"If it is your intention to set me up with a friend of Sergeant Masters, don't waste your time. I am not interested, and I advise you to stay out of my affairs," an angry Lizzy answered.

But Lydia was determined to have the last word. "As if you had any affairs."

Chapter 25

Lizzy sat with legs crossed at the ankles holding a cup of tea. Fearing that Lydia had described her as an older sister desperate for love, she had been dreading Sunday supper, but was pleasantly surprised when the three Americans turned out to be polite and eager to please, and they came with ham—always a plus.

Sergeant Masters was a beanpole of a man, but one with a sense of humor, as he informed his hosts that his height had worked to his advantage. "My draft board told me I would never see combat because the Germans would use me for target practice."

It was obvious from the way he looked at Lydia that the sergeant liked her very much, and when she said something outlandish, which averaged out to be about every ten minutes, he would look at her with the most amused look. When she mentioned his movie-making career, the one Wickham had taken for his own, he just laughed.

"My career, as you call it, consisted of standing around in a fake western town built in an orange grove near my home and one close-up shot. In it, I was clinging to my mother's skirts, crying, because the bad guys had come to town. Except for wrangling cattle for some Westerns, my career began when I was ten, and, coincidentally, ended when I was ten."

The other two Americans, Corporal Antonelli from Queens and Corporal O'Malley from Milton, Massachusetts, were in their early twenties, a few years younger than their sergeant.

"So we have both coasts of the United States represented," Mr. Bennet said, explaining that he had an interest in regional accents. "In England, because of geographical divisions created by rivers and valleys, there are many different accents, but I find your vast country produces a nice variety as well. I can hear the Dutch influence of New Amsterdam in Corporal Antonelli's speech and East Anglian in Corporal O'Malley's because that it where so many of the Puritans originated."

"If you say so, sir," Antonelli answered. "I'll have to take your word for it." It was clear from O'Malley's blank look he didn't know who or what an East Anglian was, so Lizzy thought she would rescue him.

"What did you do before the war, Corporal O'Malley?"

"I was a shoe salesman in Filene's. That's a big department store in Boston. I can tell just by looking at you that you wear a size 6B. Your mom probably wore a size 6B most of her life until she got older and her feet flattened out. I hope you are not offended, Mrs. Bennet. It happens to everyone when they get old."

Mrs. Bennet was giggling. "I am not at all offended. You are absolutely correct. I do wear a larger size now, but I thought it was because I got fat." Her remark caused everyone to laugh, and the laughter muffled the sound of the door knocker. Waiting for his knock to be answered was Charles Bingley and standing right behind him was William Darcy.

"I know they're in there," Bingley said, "I can hear them laughing. That's probably why they don't hear the knocker. I think we should just go in."

"I'm not sure I like that idea, Bingley," Darcy said. "I have never met Elizabeth's parents. It doesn't seem the right approach to pop up in their sitting room without their knowing I'm coming." And so Bingley raised the knocker once again, but still no answer.

"Oh, this is silly," Bingley said. "We'll just go in and surprise them. Jane has no idea I got leave."

But it was Darcy who was surprised. When he stepped into the Bennet sitting room, he found Lizzy engaged in an animated conversation with a handsome American, and when she looked at him, her mouth dropped open, and he wondered what it all meant.

Jane was the first to recover and was quickly by Charles's side. It was she, not Lizzy, who introduced William Darcy to their parents and their company. But after that, she really didn't know what to say because there was no formal arrangement between William and Lizzy.

Lizzy rose and extended her hand to William, and he managed to whisper, "I thought I would surprise you. It seems I have."

"How nice of you to come, Mr. Darcy," Mrs. Bennet said, interrupting the exchange. "We finally get to meet Mr. Bingley's friend."

Mr. Bingley's friend? Darcy's brow furrowed. Was that a reprimand for not coming to Longbourn sooner? The matter was clarified when Mrs. Bennet mentioned that although Bingley dined frequently at Longbourn, they had never had the pleasure of Mr. Darcy's company.

"Prior to Bingley's move to Yorkshire, I envied him his proximity to Netherfield Park as he had the benefit of such excellent company," Darcy answered. "But I see you have guests, and I am afraid I am intruding."

Recognizing the situation's comedic value, Mr. Bennet answered, "Not at all, Flight Lieutenant Darcy. The more the merrier. In fact, we were just about to have tea, so your timing is perfect."

O'Malley, who was hugely proud of his profession as a shoe salesman, repeated to the two British officers that he was employed by Filene's Department Store, a name he assumed they recognized, and estimated the size of shoes of the new arrivals. Not knowing how to respond, Bingley complimented the man on knowing his business so well.

"And you Corporal Antonelli, what do you do?" Mrs. Bennet asked.

"I drive a truck."

When Darcy heard this, his ears went up. "Miss Elizabeth, I believe you drive a truck as well. Have I got that right?"

Ah, so this is how it will be. William will make me pay for finding me entertaining Americans. "Yes, Mr. Darcy…"

"William, please."

"Yes, *William*, I do drive a lorry."

"No kidding?" Antonelli said. "I don't know any dames who drive a truck. What do you haul?"

"A lot of things." Lizzy described the different loads she had carried in her three years as a lorry driver.

"Did I not hear from Charles that you also take the local *dames* to the dances at the American base or has that changed?" Darcy asked, grinning.

"No, the dances go on, but because I have been given a different route, that assignment has been taken over by a new recruit," Lizzy said, but gave no hint of what her new assignment was.

"I deliver furniture," Antonelli said, jumping in. "Even though I live in Queens, that's one of New York City's five boroughs, most of my deliveries are in the city, I mean, Manhattan. What a pain in the butt getting through all that traffic! Do you ever have to go into London, Elizabeth?"

"Yes, actually I do."

"You do?" Darcy asked. "Since when?"

"The past few weeks I have been making deliveries to a depot in Camden. Because of petrol rationing, there isn't all that much traffic, but one has to steer clear of bomb craters."

"Yeah, London's getting pasted from all them rockets," Antonelli chimed in. "But I hear our guys took out a bunch of the launch sites, so it won't last much longer. But ya never know what's gonna happen."

Darcy didn't hear Antonelli's comments because he was digesting Elizabeth's news that she was driving her lorry into a bomb-ravaged city, and his eyes bored into her. The staring only ended when Mrs. Bennet announced that tea was being served in the dining room.

O'Malley immediately took the seat next to Kitty, who had been flirting with him since he had come in the door, and the corporal had responded in kind. Lydia sat next to Masters, but Antonelli was quicker than Darcy and claimed the seat next to Elizabeth. Before tea was over, Lizzy had heard more about the sergeant's hometown of Flushing, the New York Yankees baseball team, the New York Giants football team, and his Mack truck than she could possibly absorb.

When the party returned to the sitting room, Lydia brought the subject back to Hollywood and shared the story of how Lana Turner had been discovered while sitting on a stool in a soda shop.

"That's true, Lydia," Masters said. "But most of the young women who come to Hollywood end up waiting tables before heading back to wherever they came from or they put down roots in California and get on with their lives. For every Lana Turner, there are a thousand people who never set foot on a movie set." It seemed the sergeant wasn't shy about expressing his opinion even if it meant throwing a bucket of cold water on Lydia's quest for Hollywood fame.

"Yes, but I can dream, can't I? I mean, it can't be anything but a dream now," Lydia said, looking at her bulging middle.

"That's true. But now you'll have someone to share your dreams with," Masters said, and when he saw the tears in her eyes, he covered her hand with his. It was at that moment that Lizzy realized how frightened her little sister was. Apparently, Lydia did understand the enormity of the difficulties she would face as a new mom without a husband.

From the way she looked at Masters, it was obvious Lydia was placing all her eggs in the sergeant's basket. Although he was not as handsome as George Wickham, he was kind, practical, and had plans for a future that did not involve wrangling cattle on a film set. And he was clearly interested in Lydia. But without a crystal ball, no one could predict if his gesture was a result of sympathy or if he was truly falling in love with a girl who was a few months away from giving birth to another man's child.

Chapter 26

While Charles and Jane visited in Mr. Bennet's study, William and Elizabeth huddled in the kitchen, hugging cups of coffee for warmth. With coal rationed, Mrs. Bennet had imposed her own rationing system at Longbourn, declaring that there was no need to crank up the furnace in October. She wanted to make sure there would be enough coal to see them through the winter. No one could accuse the Bennets of being squanderbugs.

"Is it possible for you to get off work tomorrow?" William asked as soon as they were alone.

Lizzy shook her head. "There is a shortage of lorry drivers right now." She did not tell William the reason for the shortage was that three drivers from the South Midlands had been killed at a depot near Stepney when it had taken a direct hit from a V-2 rocket, the successor to Hitler's first vengeance rocket. Seeing his disappointment, she added, "I would have thought a kiss would have been the first thing on your mind."

"Not with your parents in the next room listening to the wireless," Darcy said, surprised by her suggestion.

"Oh, it is quite safe. My father would never come in unannounced, and my mother would never do anything to jeopardize a possible match for one of her daughters."

"A *possible* match?"

"Of course, they suspect we are contemplating an engagement, but I haven't said anything. Even Jane and Charles have not become engaged. Although my sister is usually not superstitious, she's unwilling to risk losing another fiancé."

"I understand her reasoning, but as for that kiss..." William said, shaking his head. "I have a bone to pick with you."

Lizzy knew exactly what bone William wanted to pick. He would want to know why she hadn't told him that she was driving her lorry into London. After what amounted to an interrogation about her new route to Camden, Lizzy responded by asking him about his last sortie.

"You know I can't talk about that."

"I don't need for you to tell me the target, but was it dangerous?"

"*All* bomber missions involve danger." But now Darcy understood Elizabeth's intent: No matter how dangerous, both did what needed to be done and went where they were sent.

"Let's not waste time by quarrelling. When do you have to leave?" Lizzy asked.

"Tomorrow. That's why I was hoping you could go with me to visit my cousin, Colonel Fitzwilliam, who is in hospital in Warwick. His regiment jumped into Holland, and he was seriously wounded at Arnhem and taken prisoner. Fortunately, he was a part of a prisoner exchange arranged by the Red Cross. My mother has been to visit him and tells me that he faces a lengthy and difficult recovery."

"Where are his parents?"

"On a diplomatic mission to Canada."

Although Lizzy understood the necessity of William visiting his cousin, she couldn't fight back the tears. Their courtship had been a series of starts and stops, mostly stops, and one in which they had spent no more than two days together at any one time. Seeing her tears, William pulled her into his lap and wrapped his arms around her. They sat in silence for several minutes before Lizzy got up and replenished his coffee.

"While I'm gone, will you be flirting with Corporal Antonelli?" Darcy asked, trying to lighten the mood. "Before leaving, he whispered something in your ear. Was it more talk about 'dames' or 'them truckers?'" Darcy asked in an American accent, but Lizzy ignored him. "I shall warn you. I have ways of extracting information."

"Such as?"

Darcy stood up and pulled Elizabeth into the mudroom. While kissing her, he caressed her breast before dropping to his knees and moving his hands under her skirt, massaging her gently with his thumbs. Lizzy was practically on fire.

"That is just one of my methods," he said, running his hands down her bare legs.

"You're not going to stop, are you?"

"It's up to you. Tell me what Corporal Antonelli said?"

"Sorry. I can't." Lizzy dropped to her knees and pulled Darcy's lips to her own.

* * *

After reaching a level of mutual frustration, Elizabeth and Darcy stopped, and she asked him for the use of his comb. "I must look like I just had a roll in the hay. It's my curls," Lizzy complained. "I swear one of these days I am going to shave my head."

"Don't you dare," Darcy quickly answered while pulling on his trousers to make room for the bulge. "In my dreams, I am always entwining my fingers in your curls. I don't want to dream about sliding my hand across a bald pate."

Darcy was about to offer to comb her hair when he heard Charles whistling, a signal that they needed to get back.

"Before leaving Netherfield, we arranged for a ride," Darcy explained while looking at his watch. "But before I go, I thought you might be interested in knowing my mother is back at Pemberley with my father, who managed to fall off a ladder while picking apples. Because he hurt his back and broke his arm, Mama is nursing him back to health."

"That's a good start, isn't it? I mean the bit about being together."

"Yes, having him at her mercy is a good start," he grudgingly admitted. "They have a lot to work out, but with my father confined to the premises and unable to play golf, they should be able to get it done."

"What happened to the ju-ju men who were living in the manor house?"

"They're gone. I'm sure they are now operating from a base in France. My mother told me that the house was so clean you could have eaten off the floor. Apparently, it was being looked after by the First Aid Nursing Yeomanry. Whenever I visited the dower house, you could see these young, and not so young, women working in the vegetable gardens near the terrace or hanging the wash or chopping wood. But I know there were agents amongst the group because I saw at least two women during my parachute training at Ringway."

"And you think my job is dangerous?" Lizzy said, poking William in the chest.

There was the whistle again. "I've got to go, and I don't know when I'll see you again. With the missions I am flying, time is of the essence, so I won't be getting any more leave."

"Then off you go," Lizzy said, putting on a brave face, but inside she was anything but.

* * *

After visiting with his cousin in a Warwick hospital and seeing the damage inflicted on London by vengeance rockets and what that meant for Elizabeth's safety, Darcy was in the mood for revenge, and the opportunity came as a result of a direct request from the French Resistance to help save dozens of prisoners who were slated for execution at a prison near the German/French border. The mission, to blow an opening in the prison walls, had been timed so that most of the guards would be at dinner when the six Mosquitoes hit the prison. Any miscalculation would result in the death of those they were trying to free, but it was understood that this was the last hope for these prisoners to escape the firing squads.

Darcy, knowing how dangerous the mission was, wrote a letter to Elizabeth, and the words flowed from the pen of a man who was deeply in love. He mentioned seeing Elizabeth at the pub in Meryton, their walk in the park at Netherfield, their first kiss, their passionate moments under a table in London and on a blanket in the Dales. He reminded her of her visit when he was floating in a dinghy on the Atlantic. There was so much more that he wanted to say, but there were other letters to write. Before sealing the enveloped, he inserted a picture his flight engineer had taken of the two of them standing outside The Shorn Sheep. The black and white photo had failed to capture Elizabeth's beauty. Even so, it was his most precious possession, and it was his intention to reclaim it.

After he had finished, he gave the letters to the mess sergeant, requesting that in the event he did not return, they be posted, and then his mind turned to the mission at hand.

Chapter 27

While removing her boots in the mudroom, Lizzy inhaled the aroma of her mother's mutton stew and was soon joined in the kitchen by her father who shared the news that there had been a massive surrender of German forces near Aachen and hoped that this meant that the war would be over by Christmas.

Lizzy was surprised by her father's optimism. The British government had said the same thing in 1914, but the war had gone on for another four years.

As soon as she had finished eating the stew, she headed for her bedroom and threw her body across her bed and was fast asleep. Sometime during the night, Jane had helped her out of her work clothes, but she had only the vaguest memory of it happening. Being in a constant state of exhaustion did have its advantages. It gave her less time to think about the total lack of communication from William.

The next day, because it was her day off, no one had bothered to wake Lizzy, and when she looked at the clock, she could hardly believe it was nearing noon. When Lizzy came downstairs, she was pleased to see Charles Bingley in the sitting room and gave him a hug. Because of a persistent problem with fluid in his ear canal, he hadn't flown a mission in fifteen days and had been granted leave. Although he was itching to get back into the pilot's seat, to Lizzy's mind, it was one less person to worry about.

She had been expecting to see nothing but smiles from the couple, but instead, she was met with grim looks. When she asked what was wrong, the two exchanged glances before Charles finally spoke.

"It's about William. It seems his plane has gone missing."

Lizzy thought her heart would explode out of her chest. Groping for the arms of the chair, she sat down and asked Charles to tell her everything he knew.

"When Jane told me you hadn't heard from Darcy for so long, I thought something might be wrong, so I called a mate of mine who is serving at Lasham with Darcy. It was he who gave me the news."

"What did he say?"

"When a plane goes missing, a certain protocol is followed. The first step is an investigation by the officer responsible for recording the after-action reports. Apparently, the flight engineer, Sergeant Mickey Edwards, had radioed the group leader that they had taken fire and were going to have to land. No eye witnesses saw the plane go down, and there were no subsequent transmissions. Yesterday, Bomber Command received a report from the French Resistance operating in that area that the burnt shell of a Mosquito had been sighted on a hillside near to where Darcy's plane had last been seen. As a result of that sighting, William and Sergeant Edwards have been listed as missing in action. Their parents have been notified."

Lizzy felt as if she hadn't drawn breath since Charles had started talking. For a moment she thought she would faint. But even worse than fainting would be to accept blindly the fact that something terrible had happened to William and his flight engineer.

"Is it possible that William and Sergeant Edwards may have parachuted out of the plane?"

"No, they were flying too low."

"Maybe they landed the plane, got free of the wreckage, and the plane burst into flames."

"Yes, that is possible," Charles acknowledged, "but there have been no reports that they were either taken prisoner or made contact with the Resistance."

"But both have had survival training. They may be on their own."

Charles said nothing. Although he wished to comfort Lizzy, he refused to provide her with false hope as too many of his fellow flyers had failed to return from a mission.

"But, Jane, you remember Jimmy Donlon. He was also taken prisoner, but the family heard nothing for three months." Instead of answering her sister, Jane looked to Charles.

"There is a gap between the Vosges and the Jura Mountains called the Belfort Gap," Bingley explained, "and there has been intense fighting there. When an army's back is to the wall, as is the case with the Germans, they usually chose not to be burdened with prisoners." Charles made no additional comment allowing Elizabeth to draw her own conclusions.

"Thank you, Charles. But I will wait for additional information." Lizzy immediately left the room.

After putting on a heavy coat, she walked out into a gray afternoon. If she remained in the house, she would have to endure sympathetic glances from Jane and other family members. Such gestures would be comforting if William was dead, but he was not—in her heart she knew he was not.

* * *

Lizzy spent most of the afternoon and evening in bed, but when she came downstairs, her father handed her an envelope that had come in the afternoon's post. Inside was a brief note from the squadron secretary explaining Flight Lieutenant Darcy's request that the letter be posted in the event he did not return from a mission. Inside the envelope was a second letter written in William's handwriting addressed "To My Dearest Elizabeth." After putting the envelope in her pocket, she returned to her bedroom but was soon joined by Jane. Sitting on her sister's bed, Jane waited for something—anything—from Lizzy in response to Charles's news and William's letter. But there were no tears, no words, only silence.

"Lizzy, are you going to read the letter?"

"No, I am not. It was meant to be opened in the event of William's death, and he is not dead."

Jane understood her sister's denial. She had experienced it herself when Lady Lucas had told her of Jeremy's death, but she had also learned that healing could not take place until the reality of the situation had been accepted. "I understand better than anyone what you are going through, having gone through it myself but…"

"Jane, I do not mean to minimize the heartache you felt when you heard about Jeremy's death, but this is different. Jeremy's tank was destroyed at El Alamein; there was no ambiguity. However, William's plane was forced to make an emergency landing. There is a world of difference between these two events. Believe me, I understand everyone's skepticism. But there is something you don't know, and because of that, I can tell you William is alive."

Jane was stunned by Lizzy's statement. Charles had spoken to the officer who conducted the after-action reports. The evidence, a burnt wreckage, no contact with the Resistance, and no word from the Red Cross that he had been taken prisoner, was grim. What could her sister possibly know that Charles did not?

"Do you remember when we first visited Netherfield Park and Charles mentioned that William had a funny story to share?" Jane nodded. "The story was about the time William ditched his Hurricat in the North Atlantic and was waiting to be rescued."

Jane had heard the story from Charles. But what did something that had happened in 1942 have to do with William's plane being shot down in 1944?

"While William was waiting to be rescued, because of the extreme cold, he suffered from hypothermia. As a result, he began to hallucinate, and in doing so, he imagined he was visited by a number of people, one of whom was a dark-haired, dark-eyed lady." Jane, who was growing more concerned by the minute, held her breath. "Because of his delirium, he was contemplating going into the icy Atlantic, but the lady in this vision told him not to do that because a rescue ship was nearby. William is convinced it was I who visited him."

Jane's mouth fell open. This was Lizzy's proof that William was not dead! She shook her head in disbelief. "Oh, Lizzy!"

"I know what you are thinking. William was hallucinating, and it did not happen. But there must be a reason why someone who looked like me visited William in his dinghy for the purpose of saving his life, and if that is the case, then why would he be taken from me before we have had a chance to begin a life together?"

"I don't know what to say," Jane said, shaking her head.

"Jane, I know what I am saying is illogical. But there is nothing logical about falling in love. Such a momentous event requires that we place all our hopes in the care of another. That, too, is not logical, but you and I have both done it."

"Lizzy, if you believe so strongly that William is alive, then I shall believe it as well. And William and his flight engineer will be in my every prayer."

Lizzy kissed Jane on the cheek. "Thank you. But please trust me. All will be well. I am sure of it."

Chapter 28

For Lizzy, her job became a means of escaping all the doleful looks from her well-intentioned family. During the day, there was no time to think about anything but driving her lorry and avoiding the detours necessitated by the massive destruction caused by the vengeance rockets. Never enthusiastic about driving into London, she now dreaded it. But in many ways, it was preferable to being at home because once she stepped over the threshold at Longbourn, she was now the most pathetic Bennet daughter, even more so than the pregnant Lydia.

"I've got a nice beef barley soup for you, Lizzy," Mrs. Bennet said in a cheerful voice which was a welcomed change from her usual funereal tone. "And I've got news as well. Lydia and Sergeant Masters are to be married at the chapel at Nuthampstead on Saturday."

This announcement was not unexpected. The sergeant had been a frequent guest at Longbourn, and during their unorthodox courtship, the family had witnessed a growing attachment between Lydia and Sergeant Masters.

"I shall congratulate her as soon as I finish

dinner," Lizzy said with little enthusiasm. After placing the bowl of soup in front of her daughter, Mrs. Bennet sat down, and Lizzy saw that her cheery façade had fallen away.

"It is not as I would have wished," Mrs. Bennet began. "When I was Lydia's age, I was more interested in dances and ball gowns, and I was flirting with every handsome young man in the county. Now, mind you, I had already singled out your father, but I was not ready to marry, nor was he. We had so much fun going to dances and the cinema or driving into town to see a play in the West End. Of course, the war came, and all that changed. But before the war, my goodness, we danced holes in our shoes. But what is Lydia doing at the same age? Buying nappies and baby bottles. You are only young once, and I'm afraid Lydia's carefree days are behind her. Because there is nothing to be done, we shall wish them joy. I don't think she could be marrying a kinder man, so we must be grateful for small favors."

After dinner, Lizzy went to Lydia's room and found the youngest Bennet showing Kitty her bridal outfit. It was a pretty ensemble Amada Thorpe had worn when she was six months along, and the pale rose would look lovely on Lydia. After congratulating her on her upcoming wedding, Lizzy did not know what to say, and after a pregnant pause, Lydia spilled the beans that Kitty was also in love.

"With Corporal O'Malley?" Lizzy asked.

"Oh, no. Not Corporal O'Malley. I was never really interested in Corporal O'Malley," Kitty answered. "But I am rather fond of Corporal Antonelli. I hope you don't mind, Lizzy. I know when he came to lunch he flirted with you, but he didn't realize you were so old. Tony's only twenty-two and…"

"Kitty, surely you do not think I am interested in Corporal Antonelli. I am in love with William."

"But William is..." Kitty did not finish her sentence. "So you are not unhappy with me?"

"Of course not. Do our parents know?"

"Mama does. The only problem I see is that Tony is a Catholic, and any children must be raised in the Catholic faith."

"Has it got to that point? You are already speaking of children," Lizzy asked and braced herself for Kitty's answer, but they were interrupted by their mother calling for help with the dishes.

Lizzy's expression had not been lost on Lydia. "She's not pregnant if that's what you're thinking. Tony is to speak to Papa after my wedding."

"So while Kitty is living in New York with Tony, you will be living in Southern California with Lee," Lizzy said. Although the thought of her sisters living so far from England made her sad, she didn't want to rain on Lydia's parade. "A part of your dream will have come true."

"Lee said that his home in the San Fernando Valley isn't that far from Hollywood," Lydia explained, "so I'll be able to visit Grauman's Chinese Theater and see where all the stars have placed their hands and feet in the cement."

No mention was made of Lee resuming his film career. In the few weeks since her engagement, there had been a dramatic change in Lydia. Her fiancé had focused her attention on the realities of her situation, and they did not include Hollywood sound stages.

"According to Lee, movie-making is not as glamorous as the magazines make it out to be. The hours are long, the lights are hot, and it takes forever to set up each shot. Instead of a film career, he will continue to work in the garage where he was employed before the war, and we'll live in a bungalow."

"That sounds wonderful."

"I know you are worried about Lee raising George's son, but he keeps telling me that as soon as he slips the ring on my finger, the baby will be his and his alone, and I believe him."

"Do you love him, Lydia?"

Lydia nodded. "I didn't at first. Lee is much more serious than most of the boys I've known, but that's a good thing in a husband. And he's very kind to me. The best thing about him is that he loves me just the way I am. You see, he was brought up in a strict home where there was little laughter. He said that's the thing that caught his attention in the first place—how much I laugh. He said that whenever he's with me, it's always a sunny day."

Lizzy went over to her sister and kissed her on the cheek. "I wish you every joy. But now I am going to bed as I am exhausted."

"Lizzy," Lydia said, calling after her, "I want you to know I pray for William every night."

"Thank you, Lydia. Let's hope God hears all our prayers."

* * *

Lydia became Mrs. Lee Masters on a gloomy day with intermittent rain showers, but the weather could not dampen the spirits of the bride and groom. Lydia laughed as if she didn't have a care in the world. While the bride spoke of her journey to California once the war was over, the groom discussed his plans to get a job at the airport in Los Angeles that was already expanding. He was eager to leave everyone with an impression that he was capable of providing for a wife and child.

Mary sent the couple a beautifully carved bowl made from the wood of an olive tree and enclosed a picture of her and her husband, Kip, on their wedding day. The couple, who were nearly the same height, looked perfect for each other. But the most endearing thing about the photo was that Mary, who declared she had no interest in frippery, had a flower in her hair. That alone was sufficient to lighten Lizzy's spirits.

All was sunshine and rainbows for Charles and Jane who had recently experienced their one and only spat. Upon learning that Charles had been permanently grounded because of chronic ear problems, Jane had been delighted. Her reaction had caused Charles's growing frustration with his medical condition to come to a head, and he had actually shouted at her. Even more shocking, Jane had shouted back that she would not apologize for being happy that he was no longer in danger of being killed. It was over as quickly as it had started, but the result was that they were even more lovey-dovey than usual, achieving a dangerous level of treacle.

220

But the surprise of the evening was when Tony Antonelli asked Mr. Bennet if he could marry Kitty. The father of the bride's response: "Dear God!" and he had walked away from the petitioner. But there was nothing shy about Tony, and he followed Mr. Bennet wherever he went until he agreed to a meeting sometime during the week.

Love was in the air at Longbourn, and as Lizzy looked out at the rain coming off the roof, she wondered if it was raining where William was or if the moon was shining brightly, and she thought of the words to their song: *I'll be looking at the moon, but I'll be seeing you.*

Overwhelmed by a sense of emptiness, she quietly went to her room and studied the framed picture of the couple taken in a studio in Skipton with a faux background of the Yorkshire Dales. While William stared right into the camera, so confident of their future together, Lizzy looked at William because he *was* her future.

Chapter 29

With nothing but hope to sustain her, Lizzy continued to do her job. As the weeks went by with no word of William, her father and mother had counseled their daughter to prepare for the possibility that William would not be coming back. Lizzy listened to their well-intentioned words, but said nothing. William was not dead. But when she returned home after a long day in London to find Lady Anne sitting in the Bennets' sitting room, her heart sank. Was the purpose of her visit to tell Lizzy that she had received a telegram from the War Office stating that William had been killed?

When Lizzy entered the room, she saw all the telltale signs of grieving. In addition to Lady Anne's red-rimmed eyes and slumped shoulders, there was a look of exhaustion, an indication of the sleepless nights that accompanied distressing news. If she needed further evidence that bad news was coming, Lizzy received it when she glanced at her parents. Although she could tell that her mother had been crying, it was the look on her father's face that was the most revealing.

"Elizabeth, your parents are the most gracious hosts. I have been here above two hours, and still they sit and listen to my stories about my son," Lady Anne began.

"I am sure it was no hardship," Lizzy mumbled, looking at her parents

"Lizzy, your father and I will be in the kitchen making a nice pot of tea. Tom, do we have any tea left?" Mrs. Bennet asked her husband, who wouldn't have any idea of what was in the pantry.

"Francine, let's you and I go and have a look."

Mr. Bennet suggested that the two women go into his study, but for the first time in her life, Lizzy wanted no part of her father's sanctuary. Would it be in that room that she would hear the news that would shatter her world? Ignoring her father's offer, Lizzy took the chair closest to Her Ladyship. She should have asked how her guest was. She should have inquired after Sir David's arm and Colonel Fitzwilliam's rehabilitation. Instead, her eyes were glued to Lady Anne, her future resting in her hands.

Lady Anne reached into her handbag, moving its contents about in an effort to retrieve what? A telegram Lizzy suspected.

"It's here—the telegram. I know it is. I'm just looking for my reading glasses."

"Why don't you just tell me what the telegram says?"

"Oh, the usual," she answered, in a voice demonstrating the level of her exhaustion. Lady Anne, who had lost a brother and two brothers-in-law in The Great War, would know what such a letter would say: *The Air Ministry regrets... Letter to follow...* "I'm looking for my notes from a conversation I had with Group Commander Granger at Lasham. Because I knew I would forget, I wrote it all down."

After putting on her spectacles, she began: *After successfully marking the target near Nancy, William's Mosquito was engaged by a night fighter who succeeded in crippling the bomber. French farmers found the... found the bodies of Flight Lieutenant Darcy and Flight Engineer Michael Edwards in the wreckage and buried them in a church cemetery near the crash site. Confirmation of their deaths was received from the French Resistance operating near Nancy.*

Lizzy went to Lady Anne and hugged her. "I'm so sorry. Your heart must be broken," she said in a reassuring voice.

"And yours as well," Lady Anne said. "I shall never forget how William looked at you when you were together in London. He was so in love."

"Thank you, Lady Anne. And I love him just as dearly."

From the calmness in her voice, Lady Anne suspected that Elizabeth failed to understand the finality of her news. As a Red Cross worker in the first war, she had seen this stage of grief often enough, but when reality hit home, it was very much like a punch to the gut. She wished to spare Elizabeth such anguish.

"A week or so ago, out of concern for a beloved sister, Jane wrote to me," Lady Anne said. "In her letter, she shared William's tale of his rescue after his Hurricat went into the Atlantic. Apparently, you appeared to him in supernatural form. Because of that visit, it is your belief that you are destined to be with William, and as such, he cannot be dead. Is that correct?"

Lizzy nodded.

"Elizabeth, you must understand that William…"

"I am sorry you are so grieved," Lizzy said, interrupting, "but in my mind, it does not make sense for me to have saved William's life only to have him lose it when we are really just getting to know each other. I am quite convinced he is still very much alive."

Lady Anne was dumbfounded and struggled for a response to such unwarranted optimism. "Do you think that if there was even a glimmer of hope that my son had not been taken from me that I would not cling to it?" No longer attempting to control her tears, they glistened on her cheeks.

"Of course not," Lizzy said, holding her hand, "but there is a higher power at work here."

"Elizabeth, I commend you on your faith, but I stopped believing in miracles during The Great War."

"You don't have to believe in them. My belief is strong enough for both off us—for all of us," she said, thinking of her family.

Despite Lizzy's assertion that William was not dead, Lady Anne felt she could not leave Longbourn until Elizabeth had moved in the direction of accepting the grim news she had brought with her.

"I don't know if I can be any clearer, Elizabeth. I spoke personally with Group Commander Granger.

There was no ambiguity in his statements. The wreckage was found. The bodies were recovered. The men were interred."

"I understand. But Group Commander Granger can only pass along the information he has been given. All I can tell you is that I know differently."

Chapter 30

Lady Anne remained with Elizabeth for two days, but nothing she said, or her family and friends said, or the vicar said, changed her mind about William. While her family waited for the other shoe to drop, Lizzy kept faith with the man she loved.

The gloom of the news about William and the cold of a wet autumn was broken by the first-ever celebration of the American holiday of Thanksgiving in the Bennet home. With the turkey and all the trimmings provided courtesy of Lee Masters and Tony Antonelli, Mrs. Bennet announced that the Bennets were living high on the hog—or at least on the turkey—and invited Sir William and Lady Lucas and the recently married Charlotte and William Collins to join them. Knowing of her family's concern for her mental well-being, Lizzy offered to play the piano, and the furniture was pushed to the perimeter so that the couples could dance. After a few dances, Tony and Kitty surprised no one by announcing their engagement.

Every objection Mr. Bennet had raised about the marriage had been answered by the young suitor. Tony saw no difficulties for an English girl from the countryside settling down in an Italian section of

Queens. "My cousin Bella married an Irish guy from the Bronx. It worked out." Kitty finding employment: "My cousin Lou owns a bakery. All the girls in the family work at Lazarra's until they have a kid. We get free bread and rolls." A worn-down Mr. Bennet had finally given his permission on the condition that they not marry until after the war had ended.

But Kitty and Tony's engagement was not to be the only reason for celebration. With Charles reassigned as a debriefing officer at a base in Lincolnshire, Jane and Charles had decided to get married. Lizzy was genuinely happy for her sister— for all her sisters. But deep within her, she was aching. A month had passed since she had received the news of William's death. Every time she received a call from Lady Anne Darcy in Derbyshire, she expected to hear that the Air Ministry had made a terrible mistake, but it was only a repeat of an offer for Lizzy to come to Pemberley, an invitation she politely declined. When she saw Pemberley, it would be on William's arm.

* * *

With the German breakout in the Ardennes on December 16, all hell broke loose at what the newspapers were calling The Battle of the Bulge. Because of dense cloud cover, no planes flew in support of the Americans fighting near the Belgian town of Bastogne, and the news was bleak. The war would not be over by Christmas.

The only bright spot was Jane and Charles's marriage. On the eve of her wedding, Lizzy asked Jane if she was nervous about her wedding night, and

Lizzy was as surprised as she had ever been in her life when she learned that she and Charles had already made love during her visit to Yorkshire.

"Charles made sure I did not get pregnant. This is *not* a hurried marriage."

"But, Jane, you are the most straight-laced person I know, and yet you…"

"Yes, I did. At the time of my deflowering," Jane said, giggling, "Charles was still flying, and I was afraid that… Well, after Jeremy was killed, I was always sorry we hadn't, and I wasn't going to let that happen again."

"And your opinion of this epic event?"

"It's a bit embarrassing at first, but then it's quite lovely. It is more than just a physical act. It is the coming together of two minds, hearts, and souls. When I was lying in his arms, I felt as if everything was good. Did you and William…?" But then she began to cry.

With William's death a reality to everyone but Lizzy, no one knew what to say. As a result, no one spoke of William Darcy at all. It was as if every memory of his presence had been erased.

"No, we did not. I was not so brave as you," Lizzy said, ignoring her sister's tears as she had grown quite used to them.

Lizzy chose not to share with her sister just how close the couple had come to consummating their relationship while lying on a blanket in the Dales. She remembered William's gently-exploring hands and the feel of his lips on her skin, and she thought she would melt from the heat coming from within her.

"No more about William and me," Lizzy said, pushing her memories from her mind. "We should be talking about Charles and you. Tomorrow is your wedding day!"

Jane, who Lizzy believed would look good in a burlap sack, proved it when she wore the simplest pearl grey suit as her wedding ensemble. As the wedding party stepped out of the church, they heard a sound they had not heard in weeks: the roar of airplane engines. As they looked up, they saw B-17 bombers streaming overhead.

"My God! Look at all those Fortresses," Charles said, practically shouting. "The Yanks will give those German bastards a pounding! Oh, sorry, Jane."

"No need to apologize. I hope they pulverize the bastards," Jane said, imitating Tony Antonelli's New York accent. Everyone burst out laughing.

Lydia, who had never heard Jane utter even a mild expletive laughed the hardest, but then stopped, her smile replaced by a grimace. Lydia was now standing in a puddle, her water having broken, and chaos ensued. It was Mrs. Bennet who finally restored order by giving everyone specific instructions as to what was required.

"Lydia, Lee, and I shall go in Mr. Bennet's car to the hospital, and the rest of you will return to Longbourn and celebrate Jane's wedding. Lizzy and Kitty will see to the refreshments, and Mr. Bennet will propose a toast. Now, we're off."

The look on Lee's face was comedy itself, but it was matched by Mr. Bennet's who realized he was about to become a grandfather. He had been eagerly awaiting the child's arrival. He thought a baby in the house was just the ticket to relieve the tension caused by Lizzy's refusal to accept the fact that William Darcy was never coming back.

Once at Longbourn, Jane and Charles were warmly greeted by family, friends, and neighbors. Lee had seen to it that the newlyweds had a proper wedding cake, and Tony had finagled a meat tray from the commissary, the spread generating more comment from their protein-starved guests than the wedding.

It was another six hours before the telephone call, announcing the arrival of Scarlett Francine Masters, came through. It was the perfect ending to the fifth full year of war.

Chapter 31

Lizzy hated January. After Christmas, Boxing Day, New Year's celebrations, and Twelfth Night, the reality of a bleak midwinter would settle into her bones. But 1945 was proving to be particularly difficult. She wanted—needed—for the war to be over so that William would come home to her. And there *was* some good news. Because the Allies had captured many of the launch sites, fewer vengeance weapons were falling on London. As a result, she had been given a new route and was driving an American-built truck with a working heater, hauling coal to dumps throughout the South Midlands.

As Lizzy made her way to the Meryton depot, she tried to think about her blessings, most especially baby Scarlett, and not dwell on the vacuum created by Jane's departure for Lincolnshire. She thought of the change in Kitty since her engagement to Corporal Antonelli. With an eye to owning her own home in Queens, she was squirreling away most of her earnings. Assuming she would end up working in the bakery owned by Tony's cousin, she had asked Mr. Cummings, the baker, if he would help her learn the ins and outs of a bakery.

While Kitty corresponded with Tony's family in

Flushing, Lady Anne penned notes to Lizzy. In her letters, William's mother wrote of walks in Pemberley's gardens with Sir David, the latest news from Georgiana who remained, unengaged, in Italy as a VAD, and the recovery of Colonel Fitzwilliam whose leg had been shattered in the jump into Holland. According to Lady Anne, although his rehabilitative regimen would have tested the patience of Job, he never complained. In addition to family news, William's mother answered all of Lizzy's questions about her son growing up at Pemberley, his close relationship with his sister and cousins, his school days at Winchester, and his years at Cambridge.

But on such a dreary day and with drops of rain dotting her windscreen, it was hard to think positive thoughts. She just wanted to get to the depot, get on her bicycle, and go home! It was not to be.

"Sorry, Lizzy," Abel Jenner, the depot's head mechanic, said. "Someone broke into the shed and stole your bicycle."

"But the shed was locked!" Lizzy said, thinking about the money she would need to replace the bicycle—*if* it could be replaced.

"Whoever did it had a pair of cutters and cut right through the lock. But no worries, I'll drive you home as soon as I've finished. You go into the canteen, and Mrs. Dickens will make you a cuppa."

Lizzy started to protest. She didn't want a cuppa served by Mrs. Dickens in a cold, dark canteen. She wanted a steaming hot bowl of soup served to her by her mother in the sitting room while she sat in her father's chair with her feet propped up on the ottoman. But there was no point in protesting. With the rain starting to turn to sleet, she would have to wait for Abel.

When she went into the canteen, she was greeted by Mrs. Dickens. While her three sons served in His Majesty's Navy, she continued to do her bit by working at the canteen. Despite the long hours, the woman always had a smile on her face.

"Ah, Lizzy, there you are. We were starting to get worried. You're the last one in tonight."

Lizzy nodded. Yes, she was the last one—nothing unusual in that. Because she was the most experienced driver at the Meryton depot, she now got the longest routes.

"Too tired to talk, are you?" An exhausted Lizzy again nodded. "Well, that's too bad because that officer over there has been waiting for you for hours now."

"What officer?" Lizzy asked as her eyes searched the tables in the darkened canteen.

"Flight Lieutenant Darcy at your service, Miss," a voice answered from the shadows.

Lizzy turned back to Mrs. Dickens. "I don't understand," she said, fatigue clouding her mind.

"It's Flight Lieutenant Darcy, Lizzy!" Mrs. Dickens practically shouted. "He's come back to you. What are you waiting for?"

Lizzy walked slowly to the standing figure. Was it really William? After months of telling herself that it was not his remains found in the wreckage of the

Mosquito, doubts had started to creep in. Questions had replaced certainty.

"Elizabeth, you have to come to me. I cannot walk to you."

Upon hearing her name, she knew it was William, and she ran to him. In her haste, she didn't notice the crutches, and she knocked him back into his chair.

"Is it really you? It is. I know it is," she said, pulling him back to her. After placing her hands on William's stubbled cheeks, she kissed him. "I believed. All these months, I believed," and she fell to her knees. With a flood of tears covering her cheeks, she rested her head on his knee.

"Elizabeth, I'm so sorry. Without endangering others, there was no way I could tell you what happened. And I don't want to speak of it right now because all I want to do is hold you." Darcy stood up, pulling Elizabeth with him, and their tears mingled.

* * *

After serving the lovers a light dinner and freshly brewed tea, Mrs. Dickens asked them to turn out the lights when they were finished and left them to it.

"You've been injured," Lizzy said, pointing to William's right leg encased in a cast.

"Yes, I got shot in the calf, and it broke the tibia. Had a bit of a problem with bone splinters."

"But you'll be all right?"

"Should be. I had surgery at a hospital in Metz. The surgeon was a German prisoner-of-war, and he put in a steel rod. Standard procedure in Germany, or so he tells me."

"Do your parents know you are alive?"

"No, not yet. I've only just got back to England. Knowing how awful it must have been for you, I received special permission to come to Hertfordshire for twelve hours, seven of which have already passed. The Secret Agent Service wants to debrief me."

"Please tell me what happened."

The original reports sent to the Air Ministry had been accurate. The Mosquito had been engaged by a German night fighter, and the Messerschmitt had inflicted sufficient damage that they had been forced down into a farmer's field south of Nancy. However, within minutes of their ditching, they were surrounded by members of the French Resistance. Knowing that a search for the missing crew would be undertaken, the Resistance had placed two bodies in the wreckage. In that way, the Germans would have evidence that the pilot and engineer had perished when the plane caught fire.

"Mickey and I had to strip down to our skivvies, so that our uniforms could be placed on the bodies of two dead Frenchmen. The men were then placed in the Mosquito, and the plane set on fire."

"There were bodies readily available?" Lizzy asked incredulously.

"Apparently, the Resistance has had more than its share of traitors. Those two men, and a few others, had been executed only minutes before our plane crashed. Knowing that the Germans would be relentless in a search for the missing crew, they loaded the pair into a barrow and brought them to the site. It was their bodies that were buried in the church cemetery. So in the end, those poor bastards ended up dying for their country."

"But why did the Resistance radio the Air Ministry that you were both dead?"

"Because of security breaches, the Resistance couldn't risk radioing London that the crew had survived the crash. If the message was intercepted, there would be reprisals by the Germans against the civilian population. So after hiding us for a few days, Mickey and I were turned over to the Maquis, men and women who had taken to the mountains to fight the Germans, and we fought with them."

"And that's when you were shot in the leg?"

Darcy nodded. "In order to avoid endangering those who were willing to hide us, we were moved along, from house to house, until the British took the village where we were hiding. Because I needed surgery on my leg, I was taken to the hospital in Metz. A week later, I was put on a plane to England. Once in London, I explained that my fiancée and family thought I was dead, and I needed to get word to them. I literally had to beg to be given a twelve-hour leave to come to you." Looking at his watch, he continued, "I have to leave for London on the next train."

Lizzy looked at her own watch. "The next train leaves in ninety minutes. How much kissing do you think we can get in in an hour and a half?"

* * *

The distance between London and Longbourn was thirty miles, a journey Lizzy could have made in her sleep, but there was no dozing off with Sergeant Masters at the wheel. The agility of the Jeep allowed him to go where her lorry could not, and there were times when Lizzy thought it would have been better if she had taken the train. At least she would reach London and William alive.

After driving William to the train station, Abel Jenner had dropped Lizzy off at Longbourn where she had awoken her father to share the news that William Darcy was very much alive. With strict instructions from William that nothing be said over the telephone, Lizzy rang Pemberley and informed Lady Anne that she should be prepared to go to London on a moment's notice and concluded the call by telling William's mother that "our prayers had been answered."

After hearing whispers outside the door, Lee Masters snuck out of Lydia's bedroom and joined Mr. Bennet and Elizabeth in the hallway.

"I'm probably not supposed to be telling you this," Lee said, "but because the bombing campaign is winding down, the Air Corps is sending the Fortresses back to America for the war in the Pacific, so there's not as much for the ground crew to do. What I'm saying is that in the morning, I can drive you to London in my Jeep."

"As long as you don't get into any trouble," Lizzy answered, "I accept."

"But while I'm gone, don't say anything to Lydia about where I went," Lee said to Mr. Bennet. "She was a wreck the whole time Elizabeth was driving into London. Since Scarlett was born, she's become a real worrier."

"Lee, you do know why Lydia chose the name of Scarlett, don't you?" Lizzy asked. Apparently, Lydia's need for a dash of Hollywood glamour had not been completely erased. Lee answered by humming the theme to *Gone with the Wind*.

* * *

Before leaving in the morning, William had telephoned Lizzy with the good news that the Air Ministry had secured a room for her at the Trentmore, an exquisite gem of a hotel tucked down an alley near the Dorchester Hotel. All during the war, it had hosted the big brass from America and the Commonwealth, but with Allied Headquarters now in Reims, rooms were available at the hotel for the first time in three years.

When Lizzy entered the lobby, she was met by Lady Anne and Sir David Darcy, who would also be staying at the hotel. When greeted by Sir David, she instantly saw what women found so attractive about the man. There was a glint in his eye hinting of mischief and a smile bordering on flirtatious.

"I am so pleased to finally meet the charming lady who has captured my son's heart," Sir David said, directing Lizzy to a sofa. While waiting for William to appear, Lizzy was so taken with the elder Mr. Darcy that she began to suspect that part of William's problem with his father was that he had not inherited his effortless charm or his natural ability to put people at their ease. In the matter of social graces, William was definitely not a chip off the old block.

With Lady Anne's eyes fixed on the entrance to

the hotel, waiting for her son to walk through its doors, Sir David kept up a running monologue, but Lizzy believed it was his way of keeping his mind off his son. Lizzy wondered if two jarring events—his wife's infidelity and his son's status as "killed in action"—had changed his life forever.

* * *

It had been so long since William had seen his parents together in the same place at the same time that he stared at them as if they were aliens, and they stared back not knowing how to approach a son they had betrayed. Finally, the elder Darcy stepped forward, and placing his hand on William's shoulder, he said, "You gave us quite a scare, son."

"Sorry. But I was under strict orders forbidding me to contact anyone. Lives could have been lost." As a veteran of The Great War, his father nodded in understanding.

Lady Anne, who had been so determined not to cry, had tears running down her cheeks, and Lizzy thought she should give parents and child a moment and tried to slip away. But Lady Anne reached out and took hold of Lizzy's hand. "There is no escaping, Elizabeth. For better or worse, you are now a part of our family."

"Yes, you are, my dear," Sir David said. "As a way of welcoming you to the Darcy family, may I suggest dinner at the Savoy?"

Before getting into a cab, William pulled Elizabeth aside and suggested that after dinner they ditch his parents.

"What an awful thing to say," she whispered. "They were devastated when they received the telegram from the Air Ministry."

"I know they were. I swear I do. But believe me, they'll understand. When my father was on leave during The Great War, he didn't want to spend time with his parents or in-laws. Besides, how can I kiss you if my parents are watching?" And he did his Groucho Marx imitation.

"What do you have in mind?" Lizzy asked.

"Nothing a gentleman could mention in public."

Chapter 32

Although it was a cold January night and a brisk wind scoured their faces, after leaving his parents at the restaurant, William, hobbled by his crutches and Lizzy moving at a snail's pace next to him, walked along the Victorian Embankment admiring the view. Despite everything the Germans had thrown at London, Big Ben still stood, as did Tower Bridge and St. Paul's and most of its world-famous landmarks. The town had survived, and so had William.

Once in the hotel, Lizzy asked William to come to her room. When William had called to tell her that she would be staying at the Trentmore, Lizzy decided it would be a night to remember. In Jane's drawer was the nightgown she had worn on her wedding night, and although embarrassing, she had asked a mechanic from the depot to get her condoms. Their time together would more than make up for her hesitation in making love when they were together in the Dales.

"I don't know if that's a good idea," William said in response to her suggestion. "I might take advantage of you."

"I'll risk it."

Once in the room, Lizzy stepped behind a screen and changed into her nightgown. It was a pale green, the perfect color for her dark hair and dark eyes. When she came out, William was peeking through a slit in the blackout curtains commenting on the fact that no rockets were flying and attributing their absence to his being in town. After turning to find Elizabeth in a nightgown revealing her lovely shape, his eyes opened wide.

"What's this?"

"What do you think?" she said, modeling her nightgown for him.

"I think you look beautiful." He took her into his arms and kissed her, but not with the passion she had expected. "This is very sweet of you, Elizabeth, but now is not the time to risk you getting pregnant. Remember Lydia?"

"Actually, I thought about that." She went to her train case and took out a brown bag and showed William its contents: a dozen condoms.

"Good God! Where did you get those?"

"From a worker at the depot."

"Well, that must have been an interesting conversation. 'I need a dozen condoms, mate. I'm spending the weekend with my lover.'"

Stunned by his statement Lizzy took a step back. "I thought you would be pleased. You wanted me so badly when we were in the Dales."

"But I wouldn't have. I would never... You're not like that."

"Not like what? A woman in love?" she asked,

deeply hurt at his rejection.

"Come here," William said, his tone softening. But she shook her head and turned her back on him, but he persisted and slipped his hand around her waist and pulled her into him. "Elizabeth, when we make love, it will be as husband and wife. I simply could not take you in that way." Silence. "Please turn around and look at me." Lizzy shook her head.

"I have seen what the war has done to women," William whispered. "Whenever I went to London on leave, I could hardly walk down the street without being propositioned, and when I was hiding in France, part of my time was spent in a brothel."

"Really? A brothel? That must have been entertaining," she said, turning around to face him.

"If you are implying that I was tempted by those girls, I can assure you I was not," he said in a gentle voice. "Some of them were so young, and they didn't look very different from the girls one would see walking on Meryton's High Street. Now be honest. If it weren't for the war, you wouldn't even consider making such an offer because you are a lady."

"If we make love, that does not make me less of a lady," Lizzy protested. "Everything changed when you went missing. I thought what a fool I was not to have given in to you when we were in Skipton. And I don't know what is going to happen after you go back to active duty, and I want so much to be with you."

"Yes, it is true; everything *did* change," he said, breaking into a smile. "Does that mean you are giving me permission to make a formal offer of marriage?" Lizzy nodded her head enthusiastically. "You know me well enough to know I'm not perfect, but I am asking you to be my wife, for better or for worse."

"No, you are not perfect," Lizzy said, smiling, "but neither am I, and I accept your proposal. But now that we are engaged, may we…"

William snapped his fingers. "Elizabeth, I have an idea. If I am successful, we shall be married tonight."

* * *

With one of his crutches, Darcy knocked on the door to his parents' hotel room. When his father came to the door, he pushed past him and asked his mother if the Darcys were still friends with Reverend John Heslip, a rector at St. Margaret's, the church where his parents had married thirty years earlier.

Sir David looked at his wife. "Are we, Anne?"

"Yes, of course, we are, David," Lady Anne said, making a face. "Why? What do you have planned, William?"

Darcy picked up the room telephone and handed it to his mother. "Please call Mr. Heslip and ask if it's too late to perform a wedding ceremony."

Mrs. Heslip answered the phone and nearly fainted at the news that not only was William alive but that he wanted to get married that very night.

"Is your husband in?" Lady Anne asked.

"He will be shortly as I have his dinner in the oven," she said with a chuckle, and Lady Anne pictured a man who was as wide as he was tall. "A wedding. How wonderful! With all these rockets and so much destruction, it will be a joy to have something positive happen. The only thing is, I don't know if we can get into the sanctuary. Will the pastor's office serve?"

Lady Anne assured her that it would.

* * *

When Darcy and Elizabeth arrived at the office of Reverend Heslip, the minister said that he had received permission from the pastor to marry the couple in the sanctuary.

"It didn't hurt your cause when I mentioned that, like Lazarus, you had recently risen from the dead," the parson chuckled while addressing William.

Although Lizzy felt the two-piece navy blue suit she was wearing was not up to the standards of a wedding outfit, it would have to do. Her only adornment was a bouquet that Mrs. Heslip had fashioned from the remnants of the altar flowers from Sunday's service.

William was making do as well, as the trousers of his RAF uniform had a slit in them to allow for the cast on his leg, but he assured her that during the ceremony he would not be married whilst on crutches even if it meant leaning up against the Communion rail.

Lizzy looked at the beautiful Flemish stained glass window behind the altar, a commemoration of the marriage of Henry VIII and Catherine of Aragon. *Well, that didn't work out very well,* Lizzy thought.

Following Lizzy's eyes, William whispered, "Catherine kept her head, so no worries."

"Thanks. That's reassuring," she said, rolling her eyes, but she couldn't stop smiling.

When the minister pronounced the couple to be man and wife, Lizzy felt tears forming. William and she had traveled such a long road to get this point. And the different William Darcys she had known flashed before her: the flight lieutenant who had tried to drown his pain in The Hide and Hare, the witty gentleman who had convinced her to forgive him at Netherfield Park, the hurt son, devoted brother, and valiant warrior. All these characters made up Fitzwilliam Darcy, Lizzy's husband.

Mrs. Heslip insisted the newlyweds and the elder Darcys stay long enough to have a slice of cake donated by her neighbor. "It was the husband's sixtieth birthday yesterday, and Mrs. Happel thought she should do something special for him. In the morning, I shall have to explain why their cake went missing, but Mrs. Happel knows I am not in the habit of pilfering her pantry."

After thanking the Heslips for their kindness, the wedding party went into a cold January night. The wind was still blowing, but it had done its job, and with the clouds gone, a brilliant sky salted with stars appeared.

"It's only ten o'clock. The night is still young. What shall we do to celebrate?" William asked, hardly believing he was a married man.

"William, really! You need suggestions?" his father asked.

"Actually, I don't."

Epilogue

With the war winding down in Europe, the British government was planning for the postwar era with an eye to its Empire. When Darcy was notified that he would be reassigned, he was relieved. With his cast off and the leg healed, he was beginning to feel guilty about sitting on his duff in an office at Lasham.

But Group Leader Granger had different plans for his pilot. Because Darcy had experience with the Mosquito, a versatile plane that would be perfect for Britain's postwar plans, he needed qualified instructors. When Darcy heard he was no longer to fly combat missions, he balked.

"Darcy, I can tell you that the last raid against Berlin has been flown. Germany is in ruins, and at this point, it is in our interest to leave as much infrastructure intact as possible because we will be an occupying army for a very long time."

"I understand about Germany, but what about the Pacific?"

"No, Darcy. You are not going to the Pacific. You have done your bit, and I shall tell you that if you request a transfer, it would be a damn selfish thing to do. Think of your bride. Hasn't she already been through enough? But I don't think you will be displeased with your assignment."

Darcy looked at his new orders. "Really? Provence? And the French are agreeable to this?"

"They want our planes because they have their own empire to protect. As a result, they have given us permission to fly missions in the South of France. My advice to you is to say thank you and leave."

Lizzy could hardly believe it. "Provence! Fine wine and excellent cheese! I hope you are pleased with your assignment because I know I am.

"At first, I wasn't, but I do have a wife to take care of, and, to be honest, I don't want go to the Pacific. I'm not one for the heat."

"Oh, there might be a problem," Lizzy said, furrowing her brow very much like her husband did. "If both parents are British, but the child is born in a foreign country, will he or she still be a British citizen?"

"I'm sure he would because...," but then he stopped. "Why are you asking that question? Are you...?"

"Yes, I am. Although I have suspected it for some time now, I went to the doctor, and he confirmed I was about two months along. It seems your assurances that using condoms every other time we made love was not foolproof. Well, you have danced the dance, and now it's time to pay the fiddler."

"Are you the fiddler, Mrs. Darcy, and if so, how do I repay you?"

"Our long-range plans are to go to Provence, but in the short term, I have something else in mind."

"Does it include me?"

"Everything I do includes you."

THE END

ACKNOWLEDGMENTS

My thanks to Jakki Leatherberry who read several drafts of this story. Her comments were critical in the development of my novel. Also, my thanks to my readers who have provided so much support for my writing efforts. You make it all worthwhile.

Other books by Mary Lydon Simonsen:

From Sourcebooks:
Searching for Pemberley
The Perfect Bride for Mr. Darcy
A Wife for Mr. Darcy
Mr. Darcy's Bite

From Quail Creek Crossing:
Novels:
Anne Elliot, A New Beginning
Darcy on the Hudson
Becoming Elizabeth Darcy

Novellas:
For All the Wrong Reasons
Mr. Darcy's Angel of Mercy
A Walk in the Meadows at Rosings Park
Captain Wentworth: Home from the Sea

Short Story:
Darcy and Elizabeth: The Language of the Fan

Modern Novel:
The Second Date: Love Italian-American Style

Mystery:
Three's A Crowd, A Patrick Shea Mystery
A Killing in Kensington (October 2012)

Made in the USA
Lexington, KY
29 September 2012